John Suckling

The Poems, Plays and Other Remains

Vol. I

John Suckling

The Poems, Plays and Other Remains
Vol. I

ISBN/EAN: 9783744711739

Printed in Europe, USA, Canada, Australia, Japan

Cover: Foto ©Andreas Hilbeck / pixelio.de

More available books at **www.hansebooks.com**

THE POEMS, PLAYS

AND OTHER REMAINS

OF

SIR JOHN SUCKLING

*With a Copious Account of the Author, Notes, and
an Appendix of Illustrative Pieces*

EDITED BY

W. CAREW HAZLITT

Second Edition Revised

IN TWO VOLUMES

VOL. I.

LONDON
REEVES AND TURNER, 196 STRAND
1892

PRINTED BY JAMES BELL, AT THE PRIORY PRESS,

48, ST. JOHN SQUARE, E.C.

INTRODUCTORY NOTICE.

A NEW edition of the remains of SIR JOHN SUCKLING, in verse and prose, has for many years past been a desideratum. The volume which is now offered to the public embraces all that is known to be extant from his pen. The account of his life which is prefixed has been reprinted from that which accompanies a volume of selections from his writings published in 1836 by the late Suffolk historian, the Rev. Alfred Suckling; but it has been carefully revised, and in certain places enlarged.

The tracts which form the Appendix are in themselves curious, and they throw some light on Suckling's history, and on the circumstances by which he was surrounded and influenced.

Some of the notes have been derived from a copy of Suckling's works, edit. 1658, purporting to have been formerly in the possession of Wordsworth. All the notes written by the poet himself are initialed *W. W.*, or signed in full, evidently to distinguish them from notes in two other hands, those of George Chalmers and John Lawson; but the authenticity of this MS. matter has (it is right to say) been called in question. The handwriting is certainly very like Wordsworth's, which varied a good deal from time to time; but it was thought that, at any rate, these remarks, whether by Wordsworth or not, could not be without a certain value.

W. W. observes :—" Suckling was among the few who read Shakespeare in that age ; of all poets he seems to have been his favourite. He not only imitated him in his writings, but praised and quoted him in all the polished circles of the day, of which he was a distinguished ornament. The exertions of Suckling to make Shakespeare popular have hitherto escaped the notice of the editors and biographers of that poet."

The following lengthy note is written on vacant spaces in various parts of the "Account of Religion," "Aglaura," &c., and is introduced by a short remark from another pen, or at least in another hand :—

" Suckling's observations on religion are always just, and sometimes profound. He has nobly vindicated the use of reason, which he very properly calls 'the highest and most golden privilege we enjoy.'" —*J. Lawson.* " Sir John at an early age made great proficiency in the ancient and modern languages ; he was also an excellent musician, at an age when music was little cultivated in England. Every poet is supposed to be a musician in his ear, if not practically. Moore, in his 'Retrospect of Prose' [?] writing in England, has named Milton as the only poet of eminence in England who was a practical musician, which is a piece of injustice to Sir J. Suckling, who was at least as great a proficient in music as Milton. Moore could hardly have erred through ignorance, because, as he tells us in his Preface to Little's Poems, he has made the early English amatory poets [?] his study, and [he] has borrowed largely from them, almost always without acknowledgment. Were it necessary, innumerable instances might be produced where [he] has borrowed hints for some of his best poems from Cowley, Donne,

Burns, Suckling, and others. Sir John Suckling, dazzled by the reputation of the French poets, imitated their style ; but he did not succeed. But he soon discovered his mistake ; he was not fitted by nature to excel in that species of writing.

"Winstanley says his poems smell more of the grape than the lamp. Suckling, Denham, and Waller were the first who polished our versification. All attempted the metaphysical style, but did not succeed. They wanted resources. Donne, the founder of the metaphysical school, had passed his life in the cloister, with no other aim but eminence in literature, and thus acquired a vast fund of learning, and by constant exercise made his hand expert at metaphysical disquisitions, of which he availed himself in his poetry.

"Cowley, his great rival, and who, though not the founder of the school, was certainly its greatest ornament, had passed his life in a similar manner. Cleveland ranks next to him ; he was also a man of great erudition, and perhaps equal in powers of poetry. His youth and manhood had been passed at Oxford and Cambridge, where he highly distinguished himself as a man of learning, an orator, and a poet. His letters possess great wit and humour, and much the same faults and beauties as his poetry.

"The Metaphysical School was formed on false principles ; its reign was but temporary ; and it was the means of creating a reaction among those who were ambitious of being ranked among its scholars, which led to all our subsequent improvements in versification and language. The school which arose in opposition is called, in contradistinction, the French School of Poetry. They proposed the ancients for their model, but found they could only imitate their chaste, nervous style of thought. The English language could not also receive their measures.[1] Recourse was therefore had to the French School, which was found more adapted to the genius of the language, and their system of versification was accordingly introduced. Rhyme, a modern invention, was deemed unclassical; but the best poets have not disdained it, and public taste has given a certain superiority to rhyme : very powerful arguments can be brought against it. The new school soon found numerous admirers, but was in great danger from the popularity of the other school. A revolution in public taste is never effected without great difficulty. Many men of learning loudly decried the new school. . . . The decision of men qualified to judge in matters of taste no doubt influenced the public. The new school would probably have fallen, but fortunately at this critical juncture Dryden appeared. He soon saw the intrinsic worth of the new school, and was not slow at perceiving the defects of the old. No man ever possessed a finer genius for poetry. Every difficulty vanished before him, and the new school was established on the firmest basis, and has ever since retained its superiority.

"For Pope, however, was reserved the honour of giving to English versification its final polish.

"I have said that the French School failed for want of resources ; but I have given an account of the other school's habits and acquirements to illustrate my remarks. As a further illustration, I must give an account of the poets called the French School.

[1] The genius of the language is so essentially different, that all attempts to introduce the ancient measures have hitherto failed. The use of hexameters . . . contributed to that oblivion in which the poetry of Sydney, Abraham Fraunce, and others is buried at present. Milton, Collins, and . . . have imparted considerable grace and harmony to some of the ancient measures, and in the present age Southey and others have attempted to bring them into general-use, but without much success."

" Waller was not remarkable for learning, and he was not early initiated into poetry. Suckling was a courtier and a wit. And therefore they may be all said to have . . . . for the metaphysical . . . , which the other school . . . , and the reputation they now enjoy has amply repaid them for the neglect they sustained in their own age . . . to say that—as their books have advanced in popularity, their . . . have retrograded in the same degree.

"W. WORDSWORTH.

"MOUNT RYDAL, *May* 9, 1838."

The play of "The Goblins," which has been inserted in Dodsley's collection, is now printed with the notes of Isaac Reed and others, as its retention in the new edition of the OLD PLAYS will probably, under the present circumstances, hardly seem desirable.

On the whole, it was thought expedient to adopt, in the text of Suckling, the modern standard of spelling and punctuation.

Considering the early age at which he passed away, and what he has left behind him in print, not to name his political exploits, it will be allowed, no doubt, that Suckling was a man of no ordinary genius, nor have we it in our power, we apprehend, to raise a better monument to him, than a faithful text of his authentic writings.

W. C. HAZLITT.

KENSINGTON, *June* 1874.

————

The edition of 1874 having been exhausted, Mr. Reeves asked me to revise the text, in order to enable him to include the work in the *Library of Old Authors*. The "Additional Notes" have now been transferred to their proper places; certain corrections and other improvements have been introduced; and the text of *Aglaura* has been collated with the original folio edition of 1638. A portrait of the poet, taken from the volume printed by the Rev. Alfred Suckling in 1836, and very preferable to that which I prefixed to the former impression, has been substituted on the present occasion.

The engraving which accompanies the *Sucklington Faction*, 1641, appears to be a copy of a French print by Abraham Bosse, after Saint-Igny, entitled *Le Tabac.*

W. C. H.

Barnes Common, Surrey,
    March 1892.

LIFE

OF

SIR JOHN SUCKLING.

IT has been observed by an author, who has surpassed all others in the path of biography, that, to write the life of a literary man with success, his biographer should not confine himself to the common incidents of life, but relate with minuteness his studies, his mode of living, the means by which he attained to excellence, and his opinion of his own works. But it is a circumstance unfavourable to him who lives in a period remote from the object of his enquiry, that sources of information like these enumerated are obtained with difficulty, and must be received with caution. To place those already discovered in the most judicious order, to ascertain their authenticity, and to weigh the respective value of conflicting testimonies, seems the chief employment of him who ventures to record the history of a man, over whose ashes nearly two centuries have rolled.

John Suckling was born in his father's house at Whitton, in the parish of Twickenham, and county of Middlesex, and was baptized there on the 10th of

February, in the year 1608–9.[1] By both parents his descent was respectable; his mother was sister to Sir Lionel Cranfield, afterwards created Earl of Middlesex and Lord Treasurer; and his father, who had been returned in 1601 as member for the borough of Dunwich, was subsequently made Principal Secretary of State and Comptroller of the Household to King James I. Under his successor, the unfortunate Charles, he retained these dignified situations, and was by that monarch elevated to the additional rank of a Privy Councillor. This gentleman, who enjoyed the honour of knighthood, was the youngest son, by the first marriage, of Robert Suckling,[2] Esq. of Woodton, in the county of Norfolk, who had represented the city of Norwich in the two parliaments of 1570 and 1585, and whose ancestors had possessed estates in that village from the year 1348.

Aubrey relates, on the authority of Mrs. Bond, the wife of one of the poet's companions,[3] that Suckling derived his vivacity and wit from his mother, for that "his father was but a dull fellow." Whether any sallies of this lady's brilliancy have been preserved, I know not; they have, at least, eluded my researches.

If Aubrey be correct, and the father excelled not in the charms of conversation, in the power

"Museo contingere cuncta lepore,"

he was certainly a man of sound judgment and acute observation. The writer of these pages possesses

[1] [His brother Lionel was baptized in 1610, his sister Elizabeth in 1612. Lysons' *Environs of London*, 1st edit., iii. 588. Compare p. xvi. *infrà.*]

[2] [Robert Suckling was Mayor of Norwich in 1582. "Cal. of State Papers," D. S., 1580—1625, Addenda, p. 80.]

[3] Familiarly known by the name of "Jack Bond;" he is introduced by the poet in one or two of his poems as an interlocutor with himself; his social qualities, however, seem to have been his principal recommendation.

letters, written by him on matters of family business,[1] in which a solidity of judgment and a knowledge of human nature are displayed in language of remarkable vigour; nor can it reasonably be imagined that, without qualifications somewhat above an ordinary standard, Sir John (the father) would have been selected by his sovereign as a Privy Councillor in times which, verging fast toward turbulence and rebellion, were already marked by increasing difficulties and open dissatisfaction.

Suckling's father, in 1602, was Secretary to the Lord Treasurer.[2] In 1606 we find him filling same place in the Exchequer.[3] In October 1604 the manor of Wansworth, county of York, was granted to him in fee-farm.[4] On the 13th December in the same year, he became Receiver of Fines on Alienations, in succession to Sir Arthur Aty.[5] On the 29th October 1607 he obtained a grant in fee-farm of the Rectory of Falmer, in Sussex.[6] In February 1619–20 he became Master of Requests; and in 1622 he was appointed Comptroller of the Royal Household, "paying well for the place."[7]

But in addition to these dignities which he already enjoyed, Sir John was also an aspirant to still higher preferment. In the "Sidney State Papers" is a letter written by Lord Leicester to his son, in September 1621, wherein he says, "It is not known who shall be Chancellor of the Exchequer, now my Lord Brooke doth give it over; it is between Sir Richard Weston and Sir John Suckling."

[1] [Many of his letters on public matters to various persons of note are in the Record Office, and two, addressed to Sir Julius Cæsar, in the British Museum.]

[2] ["Cal. of State Papers," Dom. Series, 1580-1625, p. 420.]

[3] [Ibid., p. 477.]

[4] [Ibid., 1603-10, p. 162.]

[5] ["Cal. of State Papers," Dom. Series, p. 175.]

[6] [Ibid., 1603-10, p. 377.]

[7] [Ibid., 1619-23, pp. 161, 434.]

The appointment was conferred on Sir Richard Weston ; but Sir John Suckling doubtless alleviated his chagrin by the enjoyment of a pension of one hundred pounds per annum, the patent for which may be seen in the seventeenth volume of Rymer's "Fœdera," and in which his services are recited.[1] But Mrs. Bond's estimate of the father's abilities is still further rendered questionable by the appearance of a copy of verses prefixed, amongst others, to Coryat's "Crudities," published in 1611.

It appears that the wits of the day joined in a series of panegyrical essays on that curious composition, and Sir John Suckling's muse is by no means the least entitled to commendation.

I shall not be dissuaded by the fear of incurring the charge of prolixity from inserting his effort :—

INCIPIT JOHANNES SUTCLIN.

Whether I thee should either praise or pitty,
 My senses at a great dilemma are :
 For when I thinke how thou hast travail'd farre,
Can'st Greeke and Latin speake, art curteous, witty ;
I thee in these, and, thee for them, commend ;
 But when I thinke, how thou, false friends to keepe,
 Dost weare thy body, and dost leese thy sleepe,
I thee then pitty, and doe discommend.
Thy feete have gone a painful pilgrimage,
 Thou many nights dost wrong thy hands and eyes,
 In writing of thy long apologies ;
Thy tongue is, all the day, thy restlesse page.
For shame, intreate them better : I this crave.
So they more ease, and thou more wit shal't have.

Sir John's brother, Charles Suckling, of Woodton, in a MS. now before me, thus draws his portrait : "He was a man of grave deportement and very comely person : of a fair complexion, with good features and flaxen haire."

---

[1] [In the Parliament of 1626-7, the poet's father was returned for Sandwich. "Cal. of State Papers," Dom., 1625-6, pp. 230, 231.]

Of the early history of the subject of our narrative very little is known ; nor, if it were ascertained, can it be supposed much worth recording. It would be folly, therefore, to supply by crude conjecture the channels of authentic information, and equally absurd to dwell on the relation of that precocious intellect which Langbaine has assigned him—a return, we are gravely informed, made for the injustice of nature, which had delayed the period of his birth two months beyond the usual term of gestation.

An event, however, of real importance to the interests of childhood occurred to our poet at the tender age of five years. His mother died at Norwich on the 28th of October 1613,[1] in the thirty-fifth year of her age. Whether deserving of the encomium of Aubrey or not, she was certainly a lady endued with many virtues, and tenderly beloved by her husband.

A splendid tomb, rich in statuary and allegorical sculpture, erected in the Church of St. Andrew in that city, bears an inscription to her memory, wherein her worth is recorded in terms more modest than is customary in epitaphs of that day. Amongst her other qualifications, as if in corroboration of Aubrey's statement, her mental accomplishments are alluded to in direct terms :—

" Thou wert so good, so chast, *so wise*, so true."[2]

Her husband entertained the same estimation of her worth to the last period of his life ; for in his will, dated but shortly before his decease, her portrait

[1] This is given by most of Suckling's biographers as the year of his birth ; they had not paid attention to chronological facts.

[2] [It is difficult to allow that the attribution of *wisdom* to the lady on her monument is an allusion " in direct terms " to her *mental accomplishments.*]

is singled out from other pictures which he possessed, and thus affectionately bequeathed :—

"Item. I give to my loving brother in lawe, the Earl of Middlesex, my picture of my late dear wife, hanginge in my country house, amongst other pictures, in the little roome next the great hall ; for the love he bare to my late deare wife, his most lovinge sister."[1]

Soon after the death of his mother, Suckling was removed from his father's care, and placed at a public school, though some uncertainty prevails as to the precise source of his earlier learning. If Aubrey can be relied on—and his statements of dates and facts connected with our poet are frequently very inaccurate—he was received at Westminster, but I have sought in vain for a confirmation of this assertion. The records of that establishment which relate to its scholars reach no higher than the middle of the last century, and it is certainly known that he was not admitted on the foundation. Nor are the presages of his genius better preserved, though so much celebrated by contemporary writers—a

[1] This lady had issue two sons : John the eldest, the subject of the present memoir, Lionel, who died young and a bachelor ; and four daughters. In the church of Pangbourne in Oxfordshire, is a monument erected to the memories of three of these ladies, thus inscribed :—

"Within a vault, under the marble stones hereunto adjoining, resteth the bodyes of three sisters : Martha, Ann, and Mary ; the daughters of the Right Honourable Sir John Suckling, of Whitton, in the county of Middlesex, Knight ; who died Controuler of the Householde and one of the most honourable Privie Councell unto Kinge Charles the first. Martha was first maryed unto Sir George Sowthcott, of Shillingford, in the county of Devon, Knight ; and dyed the wife of William Clagett, of Isleworth, in the county of Middlesex, Esquire. She dyed at the Bathe, the 29th of June 1661. Anne was marryed unto Sir John Davis, sonne of Sir John Davis, both Lords of this mannor, and dyed the 24th of July 1659. Mary Sucklinge dyed a virgine, the 17th of October 1658." Elizabeth, the youngest daughter, died at an early age, and also unmarried.

subject of greater regret; for the earliest indications of poetical talent are always worthy of record,
as they show how far art and study may improve a
spirit which is the inspiration of nature alone.

In 1623 Suckling was removed to Cambridge, and
matriculated at Trinity College.[1] He is entered
there as John Suckling, junior—an epithet well
merited, if we consider the date of his birth, though
he was far from being so young as Davenant relates,
who says he proceeded to Cambridge in his eleventh
year, a statement well suited to accompany the assertion of Langbaine, that "he spoke Latin at five,
and writ it at nine." A little attention, however,
to chronological facts will overset this marvellous
tale, and reduce its exuberance to the limits of
credibility. When a short sketch of the poet's life
was hastily drawn up by the first collectors of his
writings,[2] the date of his birth was inaccurately
fixed in 1613, which event has already been shown
to have occurred five years earlier. Thus his
wonderful ripeness of intellect vanishes; for, in
place of speaking Latin at five and writing it at
nine, these acquirements were less marvellously displayed at the ages of ten and fourteen. By the
same method of correcting the chronology of Suckling's earlier days, he must have been sixteen, and
not eleven, years old, as stated by Davenant, when

[1] In a letter, dated July 25th, 1678, "G. North, the
master, and the Seniors of Trinity College in Cambridge,"
request a donation from Robert Suckling, Esq. of Woodton
(cousin to the poet), to assist them in erecting a library of
that establishment, in Nevil's Court. In this letter the
college is termed "a kind of parent" towards his family,
which had "always carried a great respect to their memory."
At the back of the letter is the following endorsement :—
"May 19th, 1679. My Father sent by Mr. Brown, curate
of Wootton, for me and himselfe, toward ye building herein
specified, £120."—*MS. pen. Ed.*

[2] [Rather, by his earliest biographers, the early editions
of his writings being unaccompanied by any particulars of
his life.]

he first repaired to the University of Cambridge. Though Davenant was "his intimate friend, and loved him intirely," yet his authority on this subject is of no great weight, as their acquaintance, though it afterwards ripened into friendship, was not formed till a much later period of their lives, when the similarity of their tastes and opinions had drawn them together. Davenant, who was the son of a vintner at Oxford, where he was born and educated, could not have been early associated with a youth of Suckling's connections, who was studying at a different university.

Although much credit is given to the subject of our narrative for his eminent attainments in the arts and sciences, I should conclude with Dodsley[1] that he was a polite rather than a deep scholar. Music, languages, and poetry were the accomplishments he most cultivated, and in which he was most desirous to excel ; nor is it agreeable to the acknowledged vivacity of his constitution to imagine that more abtruse or graver subjects could very long engage his attention. Still his attainments must have been considerable, for we are told that "he early distinguished himself by the strength of his genius and capacity, which required less pains and application in him than it did in others to make himself master of whatever subject he pursued."

His facility in acquiring languages is also noticed as having been very remarkable. But while he was thus pursuing his academical studies, he received an irreparable blow in the death of his father. The knight had contracted a second marriage with a daughter of a Mr. Reeve, of Bury Saint Edmund's, an alliance which proved, in its ultimate effects, un-

---

[1] [Rather, perhaps, with Isaac Reed, the editor of Dodsley's "Old Plays" in 1780, and the writer of many of the prefatory notices. In Dodsley's own edition these are very scanty and few.]

fortunate to the interests of the poet, as much vari-
ance regarding family property arose at the father's
decease.   He died on the 27th of March 1627, in
the fifty-eighth year of his age,[1] an event which the
constitutional gaiety of the son rendered peculiarly
untoward, as the gravity of the father's character,
which was remarkable, would have operated essentially in diverting him from many youthful indiscretions into which he fell from this early exposure
to the allurements of a gay and luxurious court, to
which his birth and connections had already introduced him.   That the father entertained a like view
of his situation and its consequent perils seems
almost certain, for his will debars him from entering upon the possession of his estates till he had
completed his twenty-fifth year.

Our poet's father was buried, by the side of his
first wife, in the Church of St. Andrew at Norwich.
The poor of that city, with those of Twickenham
and Whitton, share his bounties to the present
hour; and in the former place annual sermons are
preached, which his piety desired should, like his
charities, be perpetual.   The subject of one of these
lectures shows his strong principle of reverential
gratitude to God for the temporal prosperity he
had enjoyed: he appoints "another sermon to be
preached yearly at St. Andrew's Church, on the
Sunday after Michaelmas synod, between two and
four o'clock, for acknowledging God's mercies and
favours towards him."   He died in very affluent
circumstances,[2] and bequeathed to his eldest son his

---

[1] [A good deal about Sir John Suckling the elder is to
be found in Mouro's "Acta Cancellariæ," 1847.   See pp.
277-289.   See also Ellis's "Original Letters," Third Series,
iv. 191.]

[2] He died seised of the advowson and manors of Tow-
thorpe and Wadsford, in Yorkshire; the advowson and
manors of Barsham and Rose Hall, in Suffolk, and of
Newton in Norfolk; with lands and estates in Twickenham,
Isleworth, Sion, and Lincoln; the water-mills at Nafferton,

estates in Suffolk, Lincoln, and Middlesex. His
jewels and personal effects were left principally to
his widow and daughters, and his library to his
sons, Lionel, the youngest, receiving a third part
only.[1]

We arrive now at a point whence the adventures
of Suckling's life are seen through a clearer hori-
zon : nor can this be matter of astonishment, for
the influence of birth, fortune, and person, united
to talents and elegant accomplishments, has been
felt and acknowledged in every stage of civilised
society.

In 1628 Suckling commenced his travels, being
then in his twentieth year, though Aubrey, following his inaccurate chronology, makes him to have
visited France, Italy, and Germany (and he thinks
also Spain), by the time he was eighteen. These
countries, we are told, he visited with advantage to
himself ; nor can it be questioned that his talents

in the county of York ; and houses and tenements in Lud-
gate Hill and Dorset Court, in London ; with houses and
estates in the parish of St. Andrew at Norwich.

[1] For the amusement of those ladies which may honour
this sketch with a perusal, I subjoin the following items
of Sir John Suckling's will, in which these bequests are
contained :—" I give to my beloved daughter Martha, a
fayre ring, with eleaven diamonds : and to my two pretty
twynnes Anne and Mary I give two rings with dyamonds
in either of them—viz., to Anne a ring with 13 dyamonds
in it, and to Mary one ring with 7 dyamonds in it. Item,
I give to Elizabeth, my youngest daughter, a jewell with
19 dyamonds in it, and my late wyfe's girdle of pearle.
Item, I give to my very loving wyfe all her apparell,
pearles, rings, and jewelles, which she now weareth, or
hath in her possession : save only one chayne of dyamonds,
which I lately bought by the help one of Mr. Hardnett,
a jeweller, and paid one hundred fifty-five pounds for the
same, which is by her to be repayd to my executors within
one yeare next after my decease ; unless my eldest sonne
and she agree about the redemption of the manor of
Rose Hall. Item, I give to my well-beloved wyfe my best
coach and twoe of my best coach-horses, and she to dwell
in my house in Dorset Court (in Fleet Street) so3 longe as
she remaynes my widdowe."

enabled him to study with correctness the picture
of human nature under the influence of different
religious and political creeds, though the assertion
of his panegyrists, that "he made a collection of
their virtues without any tincture of their vices
and follies," is unhappily contradicted by many
extravagances and youthful indiscretions.

But his adventures in Germany furnish the most
interesting incidents in his travels. This country
was at that period rendered an object of universal
attention in Europe by the extraordinary successes
of Gustavus Adolphus, and became yet more strongly
regarded in England in consequence of the misfortunes of the Prince Palatine of the Rhine, who had
married the only sister of the British monarch.

A commission, after many delays, was granted
by Charles to the Marquis of Hamilton to raise a
body of six thousand men, to act with him as their
general, under the King of Sweden, and in behalf
of the Palatine.

These troops embarked at Yarmouth, and landed
in Germany on the 31st of July 1631, with the loss
of only two men. Suckling united himself to this
expedition, being one of forty gentlemen's sons who
served about the Marquis's immediate person.[1] This
body of auxiliaries, it is well known, was not suffered to remain inactive, and rendered very effectual
service to Gustavus at the first defeat of Tilly before
Leipsic, on the 7th of September following, a battle
of great importance at that time, and obstinately
contested. He was also present at the sieges of
Crossen, Guben, Glogau, and Magdeburg, and obtained considerable military reputation for his conduct in several successive actions, fought during the

[1] [There is a letter from Suckling to Sir Henry Vane,
May 2, 1632, in which he gives many particulars of the
war then going on, but does not enter into purely personal
details. See it printed for the first time, from the original
in the State Paper Office, among the Correspondence.]

inroads of Hamilton in the provinces of Lusatia and
Silesia.

It is probable that he continued · abroad in his
military capacity till the return of Hamilton in
September 1632. We cannot, however, follow him
during this period of his life with the accuracy that
might be desired ; for, though several of his letters
from abroad are remaining, they unfortunately bear
no dates.[1]

On the conclusion of his campaigns he returned
to England with the character of an accomplished
gentleman, distinguished by polite learning, wit,
and gallantry. To a frankness of manners and ·a
graceful person he united an easiness of carriage
and an elegance of address so remarkable, as to
draw forth the observation that "he had the
peculiar happiness of making every thing he did
become him."

"He was so famous at court," says Sir William
Davenant, "for his accomplishments and readie
sparkling wit, that he was the bull that was bayted,
his repartee and witt beinge most sparkling, when
most set on and provoked." But if we take a short
retrospect of the national feelings and manners of
that period, it will enable us to understand more
clearly, how much a man of Suckling's accomplishments must have been valued in a court like that
of Charles I. The growing love of liberty, for
which these times were now remarkable, was op-
posed by a spirit of devoted loyalty, as magnificent
in its display as it was elevated in its principle.
The severe and ascetic habits which the popular

---

[1] [The writer here inserted a letter written by Suckling
about this time ; but it is given in the Correspondence,
and did not seem worth repeating. Mr. Suckling was not
aware that, in MS. Ashmole, 826, is a letter from Suckling
to Will (Davenant?), dated 18th November, 1620. See it
printed, for the first time, among the Correspondence. It
appears to have been really written at Dunkirk.]

party combined with their democratic opinions
served only to render them more hateful to the
Cavaliers, by whom the refined amusements and
gallantry of the court were pursued with a redoubled
vivacity, which at once gratified party-spirit, and
indulged that inclination to pleasure all find so
imperious in its demands. Literature and the fine
arts obtained an unprecedented encouragement from
the king; and these, directed by his own acknowledged taste, and by that of the beautiful Henrietta
Maria, rendered the court of England the most
polished in Europe. "The pleasures of the court,"
says Walpole, in his "Anecdotes of Painting," "were
carried on with much taste and magnificence.
Poetry, painting, music, and architecture were all
called in to make them rational amusements. Ben
Jonson was the laureate, Inigo Jones the inventor
of the decorations; Laniere and Ferabosco composed
the symphonies; the king, the queen, and the young
nobility, danced in the interludes."

In a state of refined society like this, the accomplishments of Suckling were eminently calculated
to shine: gay, witty, generous, and gallant, he was
considered, says Winstanley, "as the darling of the
court." At his house at Whitton, entertainments
similar to the court masques were introduced, on
which his poetical talents and utmost efforts were
exhausted to produce delight.

One of his magnificent assemblies, given in London, is noticed by a contemporary for its sumptuous-
ness and eccentricity, and is said to have cost him
an astonishing sum.[1] Every court lady who could

---

[1] The words of my authority are, "hundreds of pounds,"
and if we consider the value of money in those days, a very
large sum must have been thus expended. Suckling's pro-
fuseness towards the fair sex is also related in another place
by the same writer: he mentions a countess "whom he had
highly courted, and had spent on her, in treating her, some
thousands of pounds." *Vide* Aubrey's "Sketches."

boast of youth and beauty was present, his gallantry
excluding those not so blessed. Yet so abundant
were fair faces in that day, that the rooms were
overflowing, as if Nature were resolute in producing
objects of adoration in proportion as their votaries
were numerous and devoted. These ladies Suckling
entertained with every rarity which wealth could
collect and taste prescribe. But the last course displayed his sprightly gallantry; it consisted not of
viands, yet more delicate and choice, but of silk
stockings, garters, and gloves, presents at that time
of no contemptible value.

Amidst scenes like these, we may suppose, were
produced that variety of beautiful letters to the fair
sex, in which he so much excelled.[1]

But with these amusements he unhappily combined pursuits of a more odious character. He
became enamoured of play, and entered into habits
of deep gaming with an eagerness unworthy of its
cause. He distinguished himself in these, as in
more defensible gratifications, and was soon known
as the best bowler and card-player in the kingdom,
to the neglect, probably, of worthier attainments.
To his fondness for the former pursuit he alludes in
his poem of " The Sessions of the Poets : "—

> " Suckling next was call'd, but did not appear,
>   But straight one whisper'd Apollo i' th' ear,
>   That of all men living he cared not for't,
>   He loved not the Muses so well as his sport :
>   And prized black eyes, or a lucky hit
>   At bowls, above all the trophies of wit."

---

[1] [From passages in Suckling's correspondence it is to be
gathered with tolerable ease and clearness that " Aglaura,"
after whom he named one of his dramas, was a native of
Anglesey, if not one of the daughters of Sir Richard
Bulkeley, of Baron-hill, Beaumaris. A search has been
undertaken by the Editor, with the kind help of Mr.
Richard Sims, among some of the MSS. at the British
Museum, with a view to clearing up this point, but without success.]

We are told that his sisters came one day to the Piccadilly bowling-green, "crying for the fear he should lose all their portions."

As a card-player he was equally notorious, and became so enraptured with the fascinations of play, that he would frequently lie in bed the greater part of the day with a pack of cards before him, to obtain by practice the most perfect knowledge and management of their powers. In short, his notoriety became so remarkable, says Aubrey, "that no shopkeeper would trust him for sixpence; as to-day, for instance, he might, by winning, be worth £200; the next day, he might not be worth half so much, or perhaps sometimes *minus nihilo.*" [1]

But this picture is unquestionably overcharged, and must be regarded with caution, as sketched by one who has shown no tenderness in delineating his character, and who, in recording his vices, has made no mention of his sociable and amiable temper, his generous and friendly disposition; and it is further important, in estimating the true character of our poet, that no unworthy practices in pursuing this imprudent indulgence have ever been attached to his reputation. That he never seriously injured his fortune by it is certain, from the large sums of money he was afterwards enabled to expend on worthier and patriotic purposes.

Sir William Davenant's portrait of his friend and brother poet, while labouring under the influence of ill success, is worth recording, as characterising that

---

[1] [In a newsletter from George Garrard to Lady Conway, Sept. 18, 1635 ("Cal. of State Papers," D. S., 1635, p. 385), it is said : "My Lady Duchess of Buckingham miscarried this summer. I heard her husband, my Lord Dunhill, lost at the Wells at Tunbridge about £2000 at ninepins, most of it to Sir John Sutlin." See Spence's "Anecdotes," edit. 1858, pp. 2-4 : "The story of the French cards was told me by the late Duke of Buckingham, and he had it from old Lady Dorset herself."—*P.*]

elasticity of mind for which he was particularly distinguished. "On these occasions, when at his lowest ebb, he would make himself glorious in apparel, and said that it exalted his spirits, and that he had then the best luck, when he was most gallant, and his spirits high." A friendly reprehension of this vice drew from him a letter, in which he promises speedy amendment, wittily desires some other sin to be assigned him in its place, and insinuates that his attachment to it had arisen rather from a want of fitter employments than from a vicious inclination.[1]

Sir William Davenant tells us he would say that "he did not much care for a lord's converse, for that they were in those dayes damnably proud and arrogant, and the French would say that my Lord d'Angleterre look't comme un mastiff-dog." Notwithstanding this satire, we know he was sincerely attached to many of the nobility; and to the marriage of Lord Broghill, towards whom he was closely drawn by the ties of friendship, we owe the production of one of the most beautiful ballads in our language.

The preceding recital of juvenile errors has been demanded by impartiality from the pen of biography; but it more gladly records that an earnestness of purpose, alike honourable and patriotic, marked the employment of Suckling's latter years. His most valued associates were now men dignified by their virtue and distinguished by their abilities. The amiable and virtuous Lord Falkland, and Roger Boyle, Lord Broghill—a man whose character, in both public and private life, approached the perfection of human nature[2]—were his most

---

[1] [See the Correspondence.]

[2] *Vide* "Memoirs of Roger Boyle, Earl of Orrery," by the Rev. Thomas Morrice, folio, p. 49. The pen of Suckling has twice eulogised this nobleman; and Lord Falkland has received an elegant compliment from him in "The Sessions of the Poets."

chosen companions; with whom Stanley, the learned editor of Æschylus, Davenant and Jonson, Shirley, Hall, and Nabbes—writers of no contemptible merit—shared his conversation and enjoyed his friendship.[1]

In this place may be mentioned a circumstance which is not only too singular in itself to pass unnoticed, but deserves recording as a triumph of Suckling's pen, which on the present occasion reclaimed a relative from the path of folly, and rendered him an useful and respectable member of society. Charles Suckling, the youngest son of the poet's uncle, Charles Suckling, Esq. of Woodton, had for some years indulged in a strange propensity of paying attentions to very young women, whom he deserted as they became marriageable, when he transferred his love to fresh objects more juvenile, who, in their turn, were in like manner discarded.

To wean his relative from this weak and dishonourable conduct, he tried, at his uncle's request, the effects of raillery and satire—engines of very formidable calibre, of which Suckling well knew the use. In his letter on this subject which he addressed to his cousin, he ridicules him as a "founder of a new sect of fools in the commonwealth of lovers," compares his conduct to that of the jackanapes in the fable, who let out his partridges one by one, for the pleasure of staring after what was irrevocable, and with admirable sense reminds him that, while engaged in such senseless sport, the "*fugaces anni*" of life were fleeting at a rapid rate. "'Sfoot, it is the story of the jackanapes and the partridges! thou starest after a beauty till it is lost to thee, and then

---

[1] [In 1638 Nabbes dedicated to Suckling his play of "Covent Garden," and in 1639 Wye Salstonstall inscribed "To the right worshipful Sir John Suckling, Knight," his translation of Ovid's "De Ponto." See also Hazlitt's edit. of Carew, xliv.-vi.]

lettest out another, and starest after that till *it* is gone too, never considering that it is here, as in the Thames, and that while it runs up in the middle, it runs down on the sides : while thou contemplatest the coming-in tide and flow of beauty, that it ebbs with *thee*, and that youth goes out at the same time." [1]

It may be added that the wit and raillery of Suckling's remarks were well directed, as they effectually cured the trifler of his fickleness in affairs of the heart. By a reputable marriage with an amiable lady he became the father of four daughters, of whom Lucy Suckling, the eldest, by her union with John Knyvet, was ancestress of the present Baron Berners. But while Suckling was basking in the sunny regions of court popularity, distinguished as the favourite of his monarch, by whom he was now knighted, and just before his absolute devotion to literature and public affairs, a circumstance occurred of considerable importance to his reputation and happiness.

He had been for some time a captive to the personal charms of the daughter of Sir Henry Willoughby, a lady of great expectations, but unhappily possessed of a temper and disposition revengeful and coarse. The relation of this entanglement, and its unfortunate termination, are so pertinently narrated in the " Strafford State Papers," [2] that it will be better to transcribe the words of the original writer, than mar them by using my own :—

[1] [This letter of counsel is evidently referred to in "Aglaura," iv. 1.]

[2] Vol. i. p. 336, folio edition, in Mr. Garrard's letter to the Lord-Deputy, dated November 10th, 1634. [From a letter written by Ambrose Randolph to Jane, Lady Bacon (Corresp. 1842, p. 197), it might be concluded that this affray took place in 1626, and that the elder Suckling was the person implicated, not his son. But the letter is undated, and has been, no doubt, wrongly assigned to the earlier year.]

" I come now (says Garrard) to a rodomontado of
such a nature as is scarce credible. Sir John Sut-
cling, a young man, son to him that was Comptroller,
famous for nothing before, but that he was a great
gamester, was a suitor to a daughter of Sir Henry
Willoughby's, in Derbyshire, heir to a thousand a
year. By some friend he had in court, he got the
king[1] to write for him to Sir Henry Willoughby,
by which means he hoped to get her ; for he thought
he had interest enough in the affections of the young
woman, so her father's consent could be got. He
spoke somewhat boldly that way, which coming to
her knowledge, she entreated a young gentleman,
who also was her suitor, a brother of Sir Kenelm
Digby's, to draw a paper in writing, which she dictated, and to get Sir John Sutclin's hand unto it.
Therein he must disavow any interest he hath in
her by promise or otherways. If he would undertake this, she said it was the readiest way he could
use to express his affection to her. He willingly
undertakes it ; gets another young man, a Digby,
into his company, and having each of them a man,
goes out upon this adventure, intending to come to
London, where he thought to find him ; but meeting
Suckling on the way, he saluted him, and asked
him whither he was going ? He said, on the King's
business, but would not tell him whither, though
he pressed him if it were not to Sir Henry Willoughby's ? He then drew forth his paper, and read
it to him, and pressed him to underwrite it : he
would not, and with oaths confirms his denial. He

[1] [In a letter from Lord Keeper Coventry to Secretary
Windebank, Nov. 27, 1638, the projected marriage between
Suckling and the daughter of Sir Henry is mentioned, and
it is said to have been recommended to Suckling by the
king two or three years prior. The Lord Keeper also ad-
verts to the discredit which Willoughby had cast upon
himself by his conduct in the transaction. "Cal. of State
Papers," Dom. 1638-9, p. 126.]

told him he must force him to it : he answered nothing could force him. Then he asked him whether he had any such promise from her as he gave out? In that, he said, he would not satisfy him. Mr. Digby then falls upon him with a cudgel which, being a yard long, he beat out upon him almost to a handful, he never offering to draw his sword : Sutling's two men standing by and looking on. Then in comes Philip Willoughby with his man, a proper gentleman, a man held stout, and of a very fair reputation, who was assistant to this Sutlin in all his wooing business. Mr. Digby presseth him also to avow by word of mouth that Sutlin hath no such interest in his kinswoman as he pretendeth. He denies to do it : whereupon he struck him three or four blows on the face with his fist. They then cried out that they were the king's prisoners, and that they should have some other time to speak with them. This report comes quickly up to London. Sir Kenelm Digby comes to Hampton Court before the king came up : to his friends there he avows every particle of this business. Since, Sutclin and Willoughby are both in London ; but they stir not. Also Sir Henry Willoughby and his daughter are come hither, Laurence Whitaker being sent by the king for them. One affront he did them more ; for, finding them the next day after he had so used them in a great chamber of Sir Henry Willoughby's, he asked the young gentlewoman what she did with such baffled fellows in her company? Incredible things to be suffered by flesh and blood ; but that England is the land of peace."

The same authority thus continues on this subject : "Sir Henry Willoughby is come up with his daughter ; she is placed with the Lady Paget the elder, in Westminster, her near kinswoman ; and the whole business of discerning the young woman's affection is left to the discovery of my Lord of

Holland and the Comptroller, Sir Henry Vane, who have been with her, and she will have none of Sutclin."

The grossness of this outrage, which must have caused considerable sensation at court, excited the indignation of the king, with whom Suckling was in high favour. By the royal command, Digby was compelled to make very abject submission, though the nature of his humiliation has not transpired. It is certain, however, that he speedily became disgusted with his conduct in the affair, and with her for whose sake he had thus degraded himself.

The carriage of Suckling, as a man of courage, has been questioned in consequence of this affray, and indeed it seems to require some exculpation. A mystery hangs over the whole affair, which is perhaps somewhat exaggerated; for it is related that "Phillip Willoughby, a proper gentleman, a man held stout, and of a very fair reputation," that is, a man of undoubted courage, received the fisticuffs of Digby with a tameness equal to that of his friend, and, like him, offered no retaliation. That Digby was desirous of provoking Suckling to draw, relying on his own superiority in the use of his weapon, which would have afforded him a pretext for despatching his rival, appears evident. Indeed, it is almost certain that he presumed, like a bully, on his skill as a swordsman, and on the inequality of their physical powers; for we are told that "Digby was a proper person of great strength and courage answerable, and yielded to be the best swordsman of his time; and was such a hero, that there were very few but he would have served in the same manner:" while "Sir John Suckling was but a slight-timbered man of middling stature."

After this rencounter, says Aubrey, "'twas strange to see the envie and ill-nature of people to trample and scoffe at and deject one in disgrace; inhumane, as well as unchristian."

The kindness of Lady Moray, however, who entertained the highest regard for Suckling's talents and worth, restored him to the good graces of the fashionable world. She had made an entertainment for a large party of the nobility at her seat at Ashley, near Chertsey, to which Sir John Suckling was invited. Amongst the company was a lady whom he had "highly courted, and spent on her, in treating her, some thousands of pounds." Aubrey calls her the Countess of Middlesex; but he is evidently mistaken, as that lady was Suckling's aunt, and not likely to have been the subject of his gallantry.[1] Notwithstanding his previous munificence, she could not forbear her railleries on his late encounter with Digby; and some other ladies, we are told, "had their flirts." Sir John, as may be imagined, felt much annoyed and dejected by their ridicule.

Lady Moray, seeing his uneasiness, exclaimed, "Well! I am a merrie wench, and will never forsake an old friend in disgrace: so, come and sitt downe by me, Sir John." Upon this, she seated him at her right hand, and paid him extraordinary attention. Her well-timed kindness raised his dejected spirits so greatly, "that he threw his repartees about the table with much sparkliness and gentileness of witt, to the admiration of them all."

Suckling from this period devoted his talents to public business, and was much employed by his monarch, his practice on this occasion being in direct opposition to the principle which dictated

---

[1] [However, in a poetical satire by Henry Nevile, called "The Ladies' Parliament," without date, but printed about this time, we have—

" Middlesex was melancholy,
But repented of her folly;
Suckling's death troubled her much,
But since she hath had many a touch."]

his advice to another, "To persuade one that has newly shipwrecked to seek content among the disorders and troubles of a court, were, I think, a thing the king himself (and majesty is no ill orator) would find some difficulty to do." Sir John, however, now established his residence in the metropolis, which he rarely quitted, being, perhaps, as much attached by the means it afforded of indulging his taste for pleasure, as detained by the press of state affairs. But his continued residence there at length subjected him to the penalties of the law. A proclamation had been issued in the eighth year of King Charles's reign, commanding the nobility and gentry to spend a portion of their time and revenue on their country estates. But this salutary provision had been greatly disregarded; and as the evil still continued, it was thought requisite to take some summary steps for the enforcement of the statute.

Accordingly, in April 1635, an information was filed in the Court of Star Chamber[1] by Banks, the Attorney-General, against Sir John Suckling and others, "for that they holding, and having long held, places of employment under his majesty in several counties of the realm, ought not to desert their places and counties, whence their revenue ariseth; and are fit and able to do his majesty and the realm several services in their countries; and to continue to reside in London and Westminster: and the Attorney prayeth of his majesty, that he would issue a writ of subpœna that the delinquents may be called to answer for the offence at the Court of Star Chamber." It should be observed that this court was an engine of almost absolute authority, and its processes most alarming;[2] but Suckling so

---

[1] Rushworth's "Historical Collections," ii. 288.

[2] Sir George Markham was fined £10,000 in the Court of Star Chamber for striking Lord Darcy's huntsman, who had given him foul language. Morley was fined to the

greatly possessed the favour of his sovereign, that he was speedily extricated from the dangers of his situation.   He retired, however, without delay to his country seat, in obedience to the royal edict, and devoted himself almost exclusively to the charms of music and literature, till the increasing violence of faction again drew him into more active employment.   In this interval were produced his best literary performances.

In the year 1637 was published[1] his "Sessions of the Poets"—a piece of entire originality, which has been imitated by numberless writers, and which is valuable as showing the soundness of Suckling's criticisms.   About the same time, also, appeared his admirable tract on Socinianism : this piece, which he calls "An Account of Religion by Reason," though dated from Bath, was written, according to the testimony of "Parson Robert Davenant,"[2] "on his table in the parlour of the parsonage at West Kingston," and occupied him but a few days.   "It is a discourse, says an anonymous admirer of our poet, which for learning, closeness of reason, and elegance of style, may put to shame the writings of men of far greater pretensions on like subjects."   Suckling's expensive style of living is illustrated by Davenant's account of their expedition to Bath, to which place he at

same amount for reviling, challenging, and striking, in the court of Whitehall, Sir G. Theobald, one of the king's servants. Alison and Robins, who had reported that the Archbishop of York had requested a limited toleration for the Catholics, were amerced each a thousand pounds, and sentenced to be committed to prison, to be bound for their good behaviour during life, to be whipped, and to be set on the pillory at Westminster, and in three other towns in England.—*Vide* Rushworth, ii. 269, 270; Clarendon, Lansdown, &c.

Numerous other instances of judgment, equally arbitrary and severe, might be adduced. [See Burn's "Star Chamber," 1870, p. 138 *et passim.*]

[1] [Not printed, but written and circulated in MS.]

[2] Parson Robert Davenant was the elder brother of Sir William Davenant, the poet laureate.

this time accompanied him:—"Sir John came like a young prince for all manner of equipage and convenience, and had a cart-load of books carried down." The last is a pleasing touch in this lively sketch, as it shows that the love of pleasure and expense in which he so greatly indulged was balanced by an equal ardour for literary enjoyments and rational pursuits.[1]

In 1638 he published his "Aglaura." As this play was printed in folio, with wide margins and a narrow streamlet of type—a fashion then uncommon, if not altogether new—a writer in the "Musarum Deliciæ"[2] ridiculed it as ostentatious, and wittily resembled it to a baby lodged in the great bed at Ware, or to a small picture in a large frame. The piece was, notwithstanding these criticisms, much admired, and obtained for the author a poetical compliment, published in "Witt's Recreations."[3] It is said to have been the first play acted in this kingdom with scenes; such decorations having been previously confined to the celebration of masques. So greatly was its author determined

---

[1] [In a letter of Jan. 21, 1638-9, written from Wrest by Mrs. Merrick to a friend, the writer expresses a great wish to be in town, in order to witness a revival of Jonson's "Alchemist," and the new play which had been revised for the author by Suckling and Carew ; but to make up for this she proposes to fall back on Shakespeare and the "History of Women"—probably Heywood's. "Cal. of State Papers," Dom., 1638-9, p. 342.]

[2] [Edit. 1817, i. 52.]

[3] " If learning will beseem a courtier well,
    If honour waite on those who dare excell ;
    Then let not poets envy, but admire
    The eager flames of thy poetic fire ;
    For, whilst the world loves wit, Aglaura shall,
    Phœnix-like, live after her funerall."
—*Witt's Recreations*, 1641.

And in the satirical letter by William Norris, 1641, a further mention is made of this play. Though the author of that tract did not intend to compliment Suckling on his performance, the allusion evidently shows that "Aglaura" was highly esteemed. [See the Appendix.]

on bringing out this piece with splendour, that the
stage expenses were all voluntarily borne by himself.
He bought all the dresses, which were composed of
the most costly materials, the lace embroidered upon
them being of pure gold and silver.

Three prologues are prefixed to this play: one
addressed generally to the audience; a second to
the court; and the last to the king. From this
circumstance, and the known partiality of Charles
for Sir John Suckling, it seems almost certain that
their majesties honoured the first representation
of "Aglaura" by their presence. The expenses
incurred by the author on its production cannot
reasonably be referred to any ordinary occasion.
In the king's prologue Suckling has played the
courtier with success in a well-turned compliment
to the taste of Charles and his queen, which has this
additional merit, that it was deserved :—

> "Your power is here more great
> And absolute, than in the royal seat.
> There men dispute, and, but by laws obey;
> Here is no law at all, but what ye say."[1]

The power of gratifying these elegant, yet expensive amusements, proves Aubrey's observations
on his financial reputation to have been overstrained
—the result probably of false information or malevolence—and his subsequent munificence to his
prince will show unequivocally that he had never
felt real pecuniary inconvenience up to that moment. But these golden days of literary success
and felicity were not altogether unalloyed by a
mixture of those discomforts which embitter our

---

[1] [It does not appear to have been noticed that Suckling
had a perilous adventure in returning from the performance
of "Aglaura" at the Blackfriars Theatre, and was stabbed
with a rapier, which, however, did not succeed in pene-
trating the armour (or more probably quilted doublet)
which the poet wore. See "Four Fugitives Meeting," in
Appendix.]

sojourn here. An unhappy domestic occurrence excited a temporary gloom in our poet's family. His eldest sister, Martha, had married Sir George Southcott, of Shillingford, in the county of Devon, who completed a course of conjugal unkindness by the appalling crime of suicide. This melancholy event drew from Suckling an admirable consolatory letter, the manly style and sentiments of which are worthy of his pen.[1]

Lady Southcott was Sir John's favourite sister; she had a house in Bishopsgate Street, which was much frequented by him, and where Aubrey had seen his portrait, which he describes as a fine full length, painted by Vandyke, and considered to be of great value.[2] Lady Southcott afterwards married

---

[1] [Printed in the Correspondence, letter v.]

[2] This very fine performance is now at Hartwell, near Aylesbury [the residence of the late Dr. Lee]. It measures seven feet and half an inch, by four feet two inches and three-quarters. The poet is represented standing, and leaning on a rock with his left arm. On the rock is engraved, *Ne te quæsiveris extra.* The hair is flowing and red : he is dressed in a blue jacket, over which is a scarlet mantle, fastened on the right shoulder by a golden button : on his legs appear buff leather boots, those indispensable accompaniments of a well-dressed gentleman of his day, and to which fashion he alludes in his prologue to the " Goblins : "—

> " You're grown to that,
> You will not like the man, unless his boots and hat
> Be right."

He holds a folio book of poetry in his left hand, and a few of its leaves with his right. On the edge of the book is a paper, on which is written *Shakespeare.* The possession of the picture is thus traced to its present owner—Sir Thomas Lee, Baronet, of Hartwell, ancestor of Dr. Lee, married Ann Davis, daughter and heiress of Sir John Pangbourne, by Ann Suckling, sister to Sir John. As Lady Southcott died without issue, after the decease of the poet, her niece without doubt inherited the bulk of her property, and this picture with the rest of her personal possessions. The estimation in which Vandyke's works were held in his own day is evident from the following extract from a letter of Suckling's :—" And for Mistress

William Clagett, Esq. of Isleworth, and died at
Bath in 1661. In that year Richard Flecknoe
dedicated to her his play of *Erminia*.

But the increasing violence of faction, and the
wild clamours of the Scotch for a liberty of conscience, which they considered as shackled by the
promulgation of a national liturgy, broke in at
length upon the quiet enjoyments of our poet, and
disturbed the peaceful splendours of the court.

Suckling had published, it is supposed, in 1639,
but without date, his tragedy of *Brennoralt*, under
the title of the *Discontented Colonel;* it was intended as a satire on the rebels, under the name
of Lithuanians. But his efforts on behalf of his
monarch were not confined to his pen. The Scottish
League and Covenant having ended in open rebellion, he resolved on more active assistance.
Though Charles was averse to violent and san-
guinary measures, the enthusiasm of the malcontents compelled him to draw together an army
for the prevention of total disorder in his government, to the support of which his revenues were
altogether inadequate. On this occasion, when
national supplies were refused, Suckling stood
forward with alacrity to show his countrymen
the duties of loyalty at such a crisis, and with a
liberality which has never been surpassed, and perhaps rarely paralleled, presented his majesty with
a troop of one hundred horsemen, whom he clothed
and maintained from his private resources.[1] The

Delana's, we do not despair but Vandyke may be able to
copy it ; threescore pounds we have offered, and I think
fourscore will tempt him,"

[1] [The earliest news of these famous "hundred horse"
of Suckling's appears to be in a letter of Jan. 29, 1638-9,
from the Earl of Northumberland to Lord Conway, in
which the writer speaks of Suckling having then engaged
himself to the king to raise the troop "within these
three days." "Cal. of State Papers," Dom., 1638-9, p.
378.]

uniform adopted for this body of men was, white
doublets, with scarlet coats, breeches, and hats,
while a feather of the same colour, attached to
each man's bonnet, completed his attire. As they
had been selected with great attention to vigour
and manly appearance, and were well mounted
and armed, this troop was considered as the "finest
sight" in his majesty's army. The organising this
body is said to have cost Sir John Suckling above
twelve thousand pounds ; but surely this sum, which
appears enormous for that period, must have included the pay and maintenance of the men and
horses during the entire term of their service.[1]

With this reinforcement he joined the king's
army on its march to the north, which is said to
have resembled a triumphal procession rather than
a military expedition. Charles, with a vascillation
unworthy of his station and courage, still fostered
doubts and perplexity, and seemed willing by ample
concessions to prevent the effusion of his subjects'

[1] Our poet's uncle, Charles Suckling, Esq. of Woodton,
seems to have possessed a less enthusiastic loyalty. His
manor of Barsham, in Suffolk, had been charged £17, 3s.
10d. towards the support of a ship of 800 tons, manned
with 320 seamen. On the 6th May 1640, the following
cautious answer was returned to the Commissioners for
levying this tax, instead of the sum charged :—" Charles
Suckling, Esq., his answer is, that he doe not refuse to
paye, but he have no munny." Indeed, the returns of
the whole hundred of Wangford, in which this parish is
situated, are much in the same strain, and form a very
curious document, which is to be seen among the MSS.
in the British Museum. £1, 6s. 2d. only was ultimately
raised in Barsham. The remonstrances of the inhabitants
of Bungay remind us very forcibly of the complaints of
more recent days. They beg to be exempted from the
charge made upon them, as "trading is soe deade, and chese,
butter, corne, and all other ther commodyties doe yield
soe little price, as that they are not able to live, and pay
ther rents." Others say, " that in tradinge, times are soe
hard, that they can skerslie mayntayne there charge and
famylie ;" while, with modern effrontery, "others give
no answer, and are not to be spoken with."

blood. That the expedition would terminate by
bloodless compromise seemed a prevalent idea, and
Suckling expresses the same opinion in a letter to a
friend written from the banks of the Trent.[1]

On the 29th of May 1639, as these treaties had
proved abortive, Charles's army arrived at Berwick,
carrying with it, says Lord Clarendon, more show
than real force. The advantage, in a military point
of view, was evidently in favour of the Scots; for
though the English army is allowed to have been
more numerous, and superior in cavalry, yet the
Earl of Arundel, to whose command it was entrusted, was distinguished by neither military nor
political abilities. The Scots, on the other hand,
though less disciplined and worse armed, were animated to enthusiasm by the most powerful of all ex-
citements, religious fervour and national antipathy.
They were commanded, too, by officers of acknowledged reputation and considerable military experi-
ence, of whom the celebrated Lesly was appointed
general. The idle clamour of these malcontents for
a liberty of conscience which they already enjoyed,
and the pretence to sanctity assumed by their de-
signing leaders, are noticed by Suckling, who appears to have watched the progress of this momen-
tous business with foresight and penetration [in his
letter to a friend about the Scottish business, printed
elsewhere].

But while the king continued perplexed by doubts
and distressed by mistakes, his army came within
sight of the Scots at Dunse. The command of the
cavalry had been entrusted to Lord Holland, a nobleman described by Sir Philip Warwick as "fitter for
a show than a field." But to this character of military incapacity has been added by some the charge
of treachery. Certain, however, it is, that he dis-

---

[1] [Printed in the Correspondence.]

graced the king's troops by ordering a retreat without striking a blow ; or, as some have asserted, without having even seen the enemy. It is well known that the whole English army fled. Sir John Mennis, who, as a contemporary poet, was probably jealous of Suckling's popularity and literary merit, and who has shown himself inimical to him on other occasions, has thrown a stigma on Suckling's military character for this misconduct of his commander. He has lampooned him and his troop in a well-known ballad,[1] the humour of which has probably prevented a fair inquiry into the justice of its satire. Yet it must be allowed that no greater disgrace attached itself to Sir John's regiment than to the other troops, and that the playful exaggerations of Mennis's muse have alone rendered our poet conspicuous in this affair.[2] But this want of conduct was not confined to the English cavalry, the whole army labouring under a like imputation ; for Clarendon expressly states that, at the battle of Newburn, "the Scots put our *whole* army to the most shameful and confounding flight that was ever heard of, our foot making no less haste from New-Castle than our horse from Newburn."[3]

[1] ["Facetiæ : Musarum Deliciæ," &c., 1817, ii. 81-83. This is to the tune of "John Dory," which is found in "The Weakest goeth to the Wall," 1600, i. 2.]

[2] The power of satire and of poetry is remarkably exhibited in this case ; the retreat of Dunse is better remembered in consequence of this ballad than from the relation of the historian. The song was anxiously sought after by the Parliamentarians, who sang on all occasions a banter on one who was a decided and vigilant opponent of their insidious designs. Had Suckling been a character less obnoxious to the malcontents, the merit of the poem had hardly preserved its fame. [In MS. Ashmole 36, fol. 54, is an ignorant transcript of some verses, entitled, "Sir John Sucklinges Answeare." These lines, with certain necessary corrections, are inserted among the Poems ; but it is very doubtful, on the whole, whether they were really from Suckling's pen.]

[3] [In "Various Pieces of Fugitive Scotish Poetry,"

Had Suckling and his troops individually dis-
graced themselves, they would without doubt have
been rendered amenable to martial law; but we
find him retaining his monarch's favour after this
affair, and continuing with the army till a negotia-
tion was concluded with the Scots, when this cam-
paign, which was commenced in expensive preparations, ended in bloodless treaties.[1]

In the June following these events, the king's
army was disbanded, and with it, of course, Sir
John Suckling's troop; nor does it appear that he
attached himself to the military preparations made
in the subsequent season. But these treaties were
productive of no lasting tranquillity : the difficulties
of royalty had now become so urgent, that Charles
was reluctantly compelled once more to lay his
affairs before an English parliament, which he
accordingly summoned to assemble in April 1640.
It was in vain, however, that the king represented
to the members the urgent demands of his military
preparations, which the discontents of Scotland had
compelled him again to encounter; in vain did he
show this assembly that, although his treasury was
exhausted, his own extravagances or unnecessary
gratifications had not effected this inconvenience ;
that the assistance he required was to prevent the
total disarrangement of national tranquillity, and
that he expected such a supply only as was necessary for the current service. These reasonable
representations made no impression on men, the
majority of whom had sagacity to perceive that
royal authority would shortly become subservient
to popular assemblies, and who disloyally desired
it. Every effort was therefore used to drive the

Second Series, 1853, edited by Mr. David Laing, is a curious
poem on the battle of Newburn; but there is no particular
reference to Suckling and his troop.]
[1] [See further in the Correspondence.]

king once more to violent and unconstitutional
measures, with a view to undermine his remaining
popularity, and finally to procure the extinction of
his power. The parliament, thus refractory, was
suddenly dissolved, and the king's necessities supplied from the bounty of the Cavaliers, by whom
he was so greatly beloved, that above £300,000
were subscribed in a few days.

By these and similar expedients the king raised
an army of about 21,000 men, whom the Scots
again quickly dispersed. This was a situation still
more deplorable for monarchy! Without resources
to supply his state necessities, and overwhelmed
by petitions and addresses from the citizens of
London, who loudly demanded a new parliament,
Charles at length complied with their desires, and
the Commons were summoned to meet again on
the 3rd of November 1640. This was the assembly
which afterwards obtained the name of the Long
Parliament, and Sir John Suckling was returned
as member for Bramber. His talents for public
business were admirably adapted to this situation.

With the utmost anxiety he had long watched
the alarming and increasing dissensions between
the king and his parliaments, and now addressed
a letter on that pressing and important subject to
his friend Henry Jermyn, who, with better fortune
than our poet, survived the usurpation of Crom-
well, and was rewarded for his services with the
earldom of St. Albans.

This admirable composition is well known to
every one conversant with English history; its
maxims of sound policy, its correct judgment and
acute foresight, would not disgrace the most refined and experienced politician.[1] In this letter

---

[1] [See it in the present volume, printed, with a few
corrections, from the original 4° edition of 1641; the

Suckling displays a strong inclination to heal the wounds which party rancour had inflamed between the king and his people ; his allusions to the influ-ence and conduct of the queen are beautifully ex-pressed, and he points with delicacy to the necessity of her dismissing the Roman Catholic attendants by whom she was surrounded, and to whom was applied by the fanatics the origin of the existing evils. Though deploring the injustice, he admits the necessity of removing Laud and Strafford from the king's councils, as the only means of obtaining the services of the other ministers of state, and of allaying the public ferment.

It has been supposed that, as this letter was addressed to one of the king's most confidential servants, it was intended for the royal perusal. That his majesty did read it, and dwelt with con-sideration on its important arguments, seems al-most beyond a doubt, as the subsequent conduct of Charles was perfectly in unison with the advice it contains.

On the 5th of May 1641, a Committee of the House of Commons was formed to adjust certain causes of disagreement between Sir John Suckling and Captain Bulmer.[1] In what these differences consisted, I know not ; as circumstances of a much more important nature, which were brought to light on the evening of this day, annulled the prosecution of the inquiry. But it will be requisite to take a

text given in the "Fragmenta" varies, and some passages are omitted.

[1] Captain Bulmer was probably a cadet of the ancient family of the Bulmers of the north ; he appears, however, to have been a charlatan of no ordinary character. In the collection of pamphlets presented to the British Museum by George III., is an advertisement of his, printed in 1647, entitled "The Proposition of Captaine John Bulmer, re-maining upon record in the office of Assurance, London, for the blowing of a boate, with a man or boy in her, over London bridge in safety."

brief retrospect, to render this discovery perfectly intelligible.

The first steps of the Long Parliament had proved decidedly to Suckling that its leading principle was the gratification of party malice. Though he had admitted in his letter to Jermyn the propriety of dismissing Strafford from the king's councils to allay the public ferment, he had never contemplated the atrocity of the designs which were now openly avowed against him. The impeachment of that nobleman, on the 22nd of March 1640–41, had met his strenuous opposition; and when he became convinced that the efforts of himself and his party were vainly united to the eloquence and integrity of that truly great man, and that nothing could wrest him from the malevolence of faction, he had ardently joined with a few friends in a plan to rescue him from the Tower. It will be needless to remind the most superficial reader of English history that this plot was disconcerted, and that the designs of the "Straffordians" proved ineffectual: the discovery of their attempt, as related by Whitelock, is perhaps less generally known. "The design," says he, "for the Earl of Strafford's escape out of the Tower was related to be discovered by three women who, peeping and hearkening to the discourse of the earl with Captain Billingsley, they, at the keyhole of the gallery door, heard them confer about the falling down of the ship to take in the earl; and Billingsley brought a warrant from the king with two hundred men, to be received into the Tower for the safety of it; but Sir William Balfour, the lieutenant, refused to admit them, suspecting they came to further the earl's escape. Balfour confessed that two thousand pounds were offered him to consent to the earl's escape; and the earl himself did not deny a design, which he said was only to remove him to some

other castle. But Balfour was true to the interests
of his countrymen, the Covenanters, and their friends
in parliament."

Milton goes further than Whitelock, and openly
accuses the king of being a partner in this scheme,
"expressly commanding the admittance of new soldiers into the Tower, raised by Suckling and other
conspirators."[1]

But these active measures of Sir John Suckling
and his friends could not long proceed unnoticed by
the popular party, who had now obtained complete
mastery in the parliament. Accordingly, on the 5th
of the following May, the day appointed to decide
the dispute between him and Captain Bulmer, an
important discovery was made of a conspiracy (as
it was termed by the Puritans) then in agitation
against the whole kingdom.[2] The conspirators had
made arrangements, it was said, for bringing over
a French army to co-operate with the Irish troops
and the loyalists of the English nation.

The junction of these formidable forces was fixed
for the 22nd of the same month, and one thousand
four hundred barrels of gunpowder, it was further
stated, had been prepared, and "were already
loaden," for the purpose of conveyance to the place
of rendezvous by the contrivers of this scheme.

The House immediately issued orders that further
inquiries should be made into the particulars of
this alarming enterprise, and summoned Mr. Henry
Percy, Colonel Goring, Mr. Henry Jermyn, Sir
John Suckling, and others, to attend the next day
at three o'clock in the afternoon, to be examined as
principals in the desperate plot.[3]

---

[1] Milton's "Prose Works," folio edition, 1738, p. 391.

[2] "Parliamentary Proceedings," vol. i. anno 1641.

[3] [A copious account of this alleged conspiracy, with
the examinations of Goring and others, will be found in
Husbands' "Collection," 4°, 1643, pp. 215-34. There is
a good deal about Suckling himself in the depositions of

Suckling and his coadjutors, too well aware of their danger, absented themselves from the House, and were in consequence charged with high treason. This was on the 6th of May; on the 8th a proclamation was issued threatening them with the pains and penalties of their situation, unless they immediately surrendered themselves for examination; but Suckling was already beyond the seas, and his friends in concealment. The proclamation ran as follows :—

"Whereas, Henry Percy, Esq., Henry Jermyn, Esq., Sir John Suckling, Knight, William D'Avenant, and Captain Billingsley, being by order of the Lords in Parliament, to be examined concerning designs of great danger to the state, and mischievous ways to prevent the happy success and conclusion of this Parliament; have so absented and withdrawn themselves, as they cannot be examined; his Majesty, by the advice of the said Lords in Parliament, doth strictly charge and command the said Henry Percy, H. Jermyn, Sir John Suckling, William D'Avenant, and Captain Billingsley, to appear before the Lords in Parliament at Westminster, within ten days after the date hereof, upon pain to incur and undergo such forfeitures and punishments as the said Lords shall order and inflict upon them. Given at his Majesty's Court at Whitehall, the eighth day of May, in the seventeenth year of his reign."[1]

The discovery of this affair was made by Goring, with an apostasy which casuistry can defend but imperfectly in a much worse cause. He acquainted the leaders of the popular party with the secrets of his confederates, and magnified the dangers of a design which, from its difficulties, had been abandoned two months before.

James Wadsworth and John Lanyon, some of the particulars of which are curious in themselves on account of the mention of Suckling's lodgings in Covent Garden, a proposed rendezvous at the Sparagus Garden, &c.]

[1] Rymer's " Fœdera," xx. 461, folio edition.

This base conduct saved Goring, at the expense of worthier men. Percy had absconded, and with good fortune eluded the vigilance of his pursuers; though, tiring of his concealment, he soon after wrote to his brother, the Earl of Northumberland, confessing the particulars of the plot, yet manfully exonerating the king, who had been insidiously charged with abetting their schemes, from any participation in their designs. In his letter, which may be seen at large in the "Parliamentary Proceedings," he says, "Their intention was neither to infringe the liberties of the subject nor destroy the laws." "This relation I sent you," he adds, "rather to inform you of the truth of the matter, that you may the better know how to do me good; but I should think myself very unhappy to be made a betrayer of any body. What concerned the Tower, or anything else, I never meddled withall; nor ever spake with Goring but that night before them all, and I said nothing but what was consented unto by any party. I never spoke one word with Suckling, Carnarvan, Davenant, or any other creature." "Methinks if my friends and kindred knew the truth and justice of the matter, it were no hard matter to serve me in some measure."

Goring stated in his examination before the House, which took place shortly after this confession of Percy, "that the Lieutenant (of the Tower) was to have £2000 for the Earl of Strafford's escape, and to marry his sonne to the Earl of Strafford's daughter; to go over into Ireland, and send the army hither, and so to go over into France; to possesse the English army with an ill opinion of the parliament, and to make them advance to London; to deliver up Portsmouth in Master Jermine's hands, to be a rendezvous for the French and Papists, and the bishops to raise one thousand horse for that purpose."

Captain Billingsley, who had not the good fortune to escape, confessed on his examination, which was read to the members by the celebrated Hampden, " that Sir John Suckling invited him to the employment "—a mean evasion disproved by Percy. The Lieutenant of the Tower, whose evidence it was also thought necessary to obtain, endeavoured to confirm the previous statement of Goring, and magnified his own claims to fidelity by asserting that even so large a sum as £22,000 had been tendered for the earl's escape, which he had had the magnanimity to refuse.

Of the other loyalists concerned in this affair, it appears that Davenant was "taken at Faversham in Kent, was brought in a pair of oares to the House, and from thence committed to the Serjeant-at-arms." He was liberated, however, on bail, but endeavouring a second time to escape, was again seized, nor does it appear how his liberation was this time effected.[1]

[1] Sir John Mennis, whose acrimonious attack on the loyalty of Suckling has been noticed in a previous page, seems to have considered the flight and seizure of Davenant a fit subject for further satire. His misfortune forms an episode in a poetical epistle addressed " To a Friend on his Marriage : "—

" You heard of late what Cavaliers
(Who durst not tarry for their eares)
Proscribed were—for such a plot
As might have ruin'd heaven knows what :
Suspected for the same's Will D'Avenant—
Whether he have been in't, or have not,
He is committed ; and, like sloven,
Lolls on his bed, in Garden Coven ;
He had been racked, as I am told,
But that his body would not hold.
Soon as in Kent they saw the bard,
(And to say truth it is not hard,
For Will has in his face the flaws
Of wounds received in's country's cause)
They flew on him, like lions passant,
And tore his nose, as much as was on't,
They called him superstitious groom,

Jermyn and Sir John Suckling had fled with precipitation to the Continent, convinced that the court, which had shown its inability to protect Strafford, was consequently unable to shield his adherents.

The active life of our poet was now drawing rapidly towards its closing scene. Time, as it rolled in its unceasing course, brought no prospect of a national reunion, while the interdict against his safety continued in full validity. Reduced, at length, in fortune, and dreading to encounter poverty, which his habits and temper were little calculated to endure—hurled from his rank in society—an alien, and perhaps friendless—his energies at length gave way to the complicated wretchedness of his situation, and he contemplated an act which he had himself condemned in others.

Purchasing poison of an apothecary at Paris, he produced death, says Aubrey, by violent fits of vomiting. Some writers, with great tenderness to his character, have attributed his end to other causes and dissimilar means; but, I regret to add, family tradition confirms the first and most revolting narration.

The precise period of his death is uncertain, nor is the obscurity in which it remains enveloped likely to be removed. Aubrey states that he was buried in the cemetery attached to the Protestant Church at Paris; but the destruction of all public records, at the time of the great revolution in France, renders investigation on this point fruitless.

> And Popish dog—and curre of Rome—
> But this I'me sure was the first time,
> That Will's religion was his crime.
> Whatere he is in's outward part,
> He's sure a poet in his heart—
> But 'tis enough—he is thy friend,
> And so am I—and there's an end."

—*Musarum Deliciæ,* 8°, 1655.   [Edit. 1817, ii. 11-13]

It is certain, however, that he was dead before the expiration of the year 1642, or contemporary writers would not have assigned to his ghost the office of bringing remonstrances to the English nation from the infernal regions.[1]

If this chronology be accurate, Sir John Suckling died in his thirty-fourth year; "in which short space," says a compiler of a small edition of his works, "he had done enough to procure him the love and esteem of all the politest men who had conversed with him."

His death, as before observed, has been ascribed by some writers, not acquainted with, or unwilling to state, the secret cause of his dissolution, to a fever produced by the calamitous aspect of national affairs; and at Knowle House in Kent, long the seat of his relatives the Dorsets, is a portrait of him, to which is attached, in a printed volume devoted to the curiosities of that noble mansion, a tale of marvellous horror and romance. Having been robbed, says this narrative, by his valet, that treacherous domestic, on finding his offence discovered, placed an open razor in his master's boot; and the latter, by drawing it hastily on, divided an artery, which caused his death through loss of blood.[2] Others attribute this catastrophe to a nail driven into the boot by the valet, with the same intention. This is said to have happened on his arrival at Calais, after his flight from London; and that Sir John, regardless of the pain and danger of the wound, pursued the miscreant, and overtook

[1] [The latest tracts in which Suckling was mentioned are the "Elegy" upon him, 1642, printed in the Appendix, and "A Remonstrance of the State of the Kingdom," 1642, in which there are several references to the political movements of his friends and himself.]

[2] This is copied from Oldys, who, however, only mentions a penknife. That writer adds that the valet also administered poison to his master. [See further in Spence's "Anecdotes," 1858, p. 3; and *Notes and Queries*, Second Series, i. 172, 316.]

him. There may, perhaps, be some foundation for this story; but the horrid plan was certainly not the cause of his death.

Dreadful as is the contemplation of such atrocity, it would still be less appalling to moral feeling, had either of these narrations been correct; but truth inflicts the painful task on his biographer to deny their authenticity, and close the last page of his history with the relation of an act at once the most grievous and indefensible.

Thus perished immaturely, and in a land of strangers, the accomplished subject of this memoir; marked indeed by early levity and indiscretions, but happily more distinguished by devoted loyalty and intellectual refinement. If he be charged with want of prudence in the direction of his great abilities to his own advancement, they were at least ever exerted in favour of the learned and the deserving. If his earlier years were stained by habits of intemperance and frivolity, he has amply redeemed himself by the exertions of his maturer age. To a kind and amiable temper he united a generous and a friendly disposition; while the proofs of his patriotism and loyalty have been so fully developed in the progress of this essay, that, with all his imperfections, he is entitled to rank with the most distinguished characters of his day.

In person he was of the middle size, though but slightly made, with a winning and graceful carriage, and noble features. From Aubrey we have his picture touched with all the vigour of an original portrait: "Sir John Suckling was of middle stature and slight strength; brisque round eie, reddish fac't, and red nosed (ill liver); his head not very big; his hayre a kind of sand colour; his beard turn'd up naturally, so that he had a brisk and graceful looke."

The pencil of Vandyke is said to have produced

three portraits of this gentleman; one of which, a noble and masterly performance in the writer's possession, has been engraved for this work. A second, the fine full-length, formerly the property of the poet's sister, Lady Southcott, has been noticed in a preceding page. Of the third picture the history is somewhat obscure. For many years a portrait has been shown at Hampton Court as that of the poet Suckling, and ascribed to the talent of Vandyke. It has, however, been discovered to be, in reality, the work of Hanneman, and to represent Peter Oliver the painter. The genuine painting is therefore to be sought elsewhere.[1] There is also a portrait of Suckling in the Ashmolean Library at Oxford; whether an original or not, is uncertain.[2]

Sir John Suckling died unmarried.

The talents and satire, which he had always exercised without restraint against puritanism and faction, had rendered Suckling peculiarly odious to the Parliamentarians. The lampoon of Sir John Mennis, on his "most warlike preparations for the Scottish warre," became with them a favourite song; and a ballad, arranged in a similar metre, made its appearance very shortly after his flight, entitled, "A letter sent by Sir John Suckling from France, deploring his sad estate and flight, with a discoverie of the plot and conspiracie intended by him and his adherents against England." This [which is supposed to have been written by one William Norris[3]] was printed in London, though dated from Paris, June 16th, 1641, and recites with burlesque

---

[1] The cicerones of the place must surely have confounded the poet with his father. The portrait in question bears no resemblance to the features of the former, but is somewhat, in its general character, like the elder knight. In the collection of family pictures at Woodton is a portrait of the father in his Privy Councillor's robes, painted by Cornelius Jansen, in his very best style.

[2] [An engraving of it accompanies the present edition.]

[3] [*Notes and Queries*, Second Series, xi. 204.]

gravity the principal events of our poet's life.[1] It had proved far more valuable at the present day had it thrown any light on Suckling's closing scenes.

A pamphlet in prose was also printed in 1641, called "Newes from Sir John Sucklin, being a relation of his conversion from a papist to a protestant, &c."[2] This, which is altogether a fictitious performance of the Puritans, charges him with having lived as a "Romanist, and a treacherous and disloyal subject." This accusation probably arose from the tender manner in which he had alluded to the conduct of the queen and her Catholic attendants in his letter to Jermyn. It affords, however, one gleam more of Suckling's setting sun, as it states incidentally that he continued some time at Rouen after his flight to France, previously to his proceeding to Paris.

But puritanical malignity was not yet exhausted: a large folio sheet was printed, in the centre of which an engraving represents two Cavaliers in the splendid dress and flowing hair so offensive to the Roundheads: they are surrounded with dice and drinking-cups, as emblems of debauchery and profusion; while the paper, which is closely printed, condemns in strong language, interlarded with an abundance of scriptural illustrations and texts, all evil practices and conversation.

This curious production—which is launched against the *levities* of Suckling's youthful days—is entitled, "*The Sucklington Faction, or Suckling's Roaring Boyes*."[3] In 1642, and immediately after Sir John's death, was published a fourth performance, termed, "A copy of two remonstrances brought over the river Stix in Caron's ferry-boate, by the ghost of Sir John Suckling."[4]

---

[1] [See it in the Appendix.]
[2] [Also included in the Appendix.]
[3] [Inserted in the Appendix.]
[4] [This did not seem worth a place in the Appendix.]

These are strong testimonies of the importance attached to the political talents and sagacity of Suckling; for, had he not rendered himself an object of admiration to his friends, and of detestation to his opponents, his name had ceased to interest with the close of his life.

As a writer Sir John Suckling will command admiration, so long as a taste for whatever is delicate and natural in poetry shall remain. His works are the production of a genius truly poetic and original: his language is animated and forcible; his versification, for the age, smooth and flowing; the structure of his stanzas is simple, and occasionally novel, being founded apparently in some instances on Italian models. In descriptions of feminine grace and beauty he is peculiarly happy, and in his prose compositions is clear, nervous, and sparkling.

If we bring his poems to the test of comparison with succeeding writers, notwithstanding the continued progress of elegant literature since his day, the result will prove that in the higher species of poetry he remains unrivalled.[1] Had his name been unknown in any other department of literature,

---

[1] [In Spence's "Anecdotes" it is said: "Considering the manner of writing then in fashion, the purity of Sir John Suckling's style is quite surprising." Hazlitt observes: "Sir John Suckling is one of the most piquant and attractive of the minor poets. He has fancy, wit, humour, descriptive talent, the highest elegance, perfect ease, a familiar style, and a pleasing versification. He has combined these in his ballad 'On a Wedding,' which is a masterpiece of sportive gaiety and good humour. His genius was confined entirely to the light and agreeable" ("Select British Poets," 1824 p. vi.). But putting out of the question his merits as a poet, Suckling's qualifications as a letter-writer were very high; his extant correspondence is remarkable for the justness of his remarks, the solidity and accuracy of his judgment, the happiness of his figures, and the ease and sparkle of his style; and had he been spared longer, and it had been his ambition, we feel sure that he would have shone as brightly in politics as in literature.]

or unconnected with any historical associations, his
ballads and songs alone would render his fame
imperishable.   In applying metaphysics to poetry,
a style of writing very fashionable in his day, but
to which he has rarely, though occasionally, stooped,
he has employed his conceptions with considerable
ingenuity, nor has he allowed his ideas to overstep
the limits of propriety.   In the following stanza,
taken from his " Love's World," these remarks will
be found, I think, to apply with justness; nor can
very strong objections be made to the comparisons
employed in the remaining verses—

> " The sea's my mind, which calm would be,
>   Were it from winds, my passions, free ;
>   But, out, alas ! no sea I find
>   Is troubled like a lover's mind.
>   Within it rocks and shallows be,
>   Despair and fond credulity."

But lest the writer's judgment should be considered as warped by prepossession in his favour,
a few testimonies of others, better qualified than
himself to appreciate the merits of composition, are
adduced.

" The grace and elegance of his songs and ballads,"
says Mr. Ellis, " are inimitable."   " They have a
pretty touch," says Phillips, " of a gentle spirit,
and seem to savour more of the grape than lamp."
And Mr. Lloyd, in his " Memoirs, &c.," has the
following discriminative remarks : — " His poems
are clean, sprightly, and natural—his discourses
full and convincing—his plays well-humoured and
taking—his letters fragrant and sparkling."   A
writer in the *British Critic* observes, that " if these
models had been more frequently and more happily
copied, the French would not have been unrivalled
in light poetry."

In his prose compositions Suckling has been
equally admired; his letters are full of wit, spirit,

and gallantry, and have been rarely surpassed. His "Account of Religion by Reason," and his letter to Jermyn, prove his ability to reason with closeness, and compose with nervous elegance.

He fails most as a dramatist, though Phillips, says his plays continued to draw audiences to the theatres in his days. They did not, however, long retain popularity. Nor is this surprising; for the genius of Suckling nowhere appears to so little advantage as in his plays. Besides bearing very evident marks of crudity in the plans and hurry in the execution, they are marred by the recurrence of trifling incidents, which distract the attention from the development of the main catastrophe, and fritter it into littleness and poverty of effect. They are deficient, moreover, in that sweetness of versification and originality of thought which elsewhere distinguish his compositions; and the gleams of fire and intellect which occasionally warm us in their perusal are obscured too frequently by tedious pages of prolix declamation.

His plays are but four. Of these, "The Sad One" is an unfinished tragedy, which, if completed in the style of the four acts left us by the author, could scarcely have entertained an audience at any time. The compilers of the "Biographia Dramatica," however, consider it as showing the hand of a master; yet it possesses, in the opinion of the writer, a complicated machinery, great plotting, and much bloodshed—smoke, in fact, but no fire—violent death in the very opening scene is afterwards repeated without sufficient reason. The scenes, too, are abrupt, and the language poor. The best lines, as might be expected from Suckling's known talents that way, are contained in the little song sung by Florelio's page in the fourth act—

" Hast thou seen the down i' th' air
When wanton blasts have toss'd it ? " &c.

As usual, Suckling is most successful in his descriptions of feminine grace; describing Francelia's beauty, he says—

> "She has an eye, round as a globe,
>   And black as jet; so full of majesty and life,
>   That when it most denies, it most invites.
>   Her lips are gently swell'd unto   .
>   Some blushing cherry, that hath newly tasted
>   The dew from heaven."

In the fourth act, Signor Multicarni and his assistants are introduced for no other purpose, it would appear, than as vehicles for a stroke of satire against lawyers. After appropriating to certain performers their several parts, he exclaims—

> "But who shall act the honest lawyer?
>   'Tis a hard part that!"

The simile of comparing Clarimont's counsel to

> "Smith's water flung upon coals
> Which more inflames,"

is original, I believe, though not elegant.

"Aglaura" was, I fancy, Suckling's favourite play; and it is so contrived that by adopting either of two fifth acts, it can be represented as a tragedy or a comedy. The splendour with which it was first brought out has been noticed in a former page. It is certainly better conceived, and written with more spirit, than "The Sad One," though, as a tragedy, it is scarcely less bloody. But scenes of theatrical horror were witnessed in those days with greater delight than in our own; and Shakespeare's bloodiest exhibitions in "Hamlet" or "Macbeth" were then regarded with more than mere complacency. Suckling is, therefore, so far defensible; for he wrote in accordance with the taste of his age. The plan of "Aglaura," however, is not only very similar to that of "The Sad One," but it contains many ideas and entire sentences which occur in the latter;

though "Aglaura," it is to be remembered, was the original play.

Like Shakespeare, Sir John is very fond of concluding his scenes with couplets. When acted as a tragedy, this piece should not have been protracted after the death of Aglaura. Like "The Sad One," it contains many lines descriptive of feminine charms —a subject on which Sir John seems ever willing to dwell—

> "Lips
> Perfum'd by breath, sweet as the bean's first blossom."

In the opening scene of the first act, and in the first scene of the fourth act, are ideas which Suckling's familiarity with courts had probably suggested—

> "We are envy's mark, and court-eyes carry far."
> "Court friendship
> Is like a cable, that in storms is ever cut."

In the fourth act is a fine dialogue between Semanthe and Iolas.

The address of Orbella to the corpse of Ariaspes is full of pathos and sensibility, and not unworthy of Shakespeare himself.

The plan of "Aglaura" has been followed by Sir Robert Howard in his "Vestal Virgin;" while Pope has without acknowledgment transferred Suckling's ideas, in several instances, from these plays to his own poetry.[1]

---

[1] "But, as when an authentic watch is shown,
Each man winds up, and rectifies his own,
So in our very judgments."
   —*Epilogue to "Aglaura."*

"'Tis with our judgments as our watches, none
Go just alike, yet each believes his own."
   —*Pope's "Essay on Criticism."*

"High characters, cries one, and he would see
Things that ne'er were, nor are, nor e'er will be."
   —*Epilogue to "The Goblins."*

The vivacity of Suckling's mind promised better success from his attempts in comedy; yet "The Goblins," it must be confessed, possesses little merit. The idea of the play is evidently borrowed from Shakespeare; and the same arguments may be advanced in defence of the machinery adopted in it as have been so powerfully adduced by Dr. Johnson in support of Shakespeare's employment of witches in "Macbeth." A belief in the agency of witchcraft was still an universal notion in Suckling's time—nay, it had been rendered a fashionable illusion by the publication of King James's work on demonology. The curious expression which occurs in this play—

> "The Sedgly curse upon thee,
> And the great fiend ride through thee
> Booted and spurr'd, with a scythe on his neck,"

is mentioned by Howell.[1]

In the second song in the third act is an extraordinary line—

> "The prince of darkness is a gentleman."

The Lady Juliana Barnes uses an expression very similar—

> "Jesus was a gentleman."

"Brennoralt" I consider Suckling's best play, and it might with little alteration be adapted to modern taste. The dialogue is more lively, and the plot less complicated and bloody, than in his other tragedies. It abounds in allusions to the existing state of public affairs, and has been thought to point in some places to his own situation. When he says the court is

> "A most eternal place of low affronts,
> And then as low submissions,"

the conduct and humiliation of Digby were, probably,

> "Whoever thinks a faultless piece to see,
> Thinks what ne'er was, nor is, nor e'er shall be."
> —*Pope's "Essay on Criticism."*

[1] [See Hazlitt's "Proverbs," 1869, p. 365.]

in the author's recollection. In the beginning of the
third act he introduces the king in conversation with
Brennoralt and his councillors, which affords an opportunity of discussing the subjects then in agitation between Charles and the Scots. The passage is
too long to be repeated in this place, particularly as
it will be found in the body of this volume ; but it
is worthy of an attentive perusal. The play contains
many excellent strokes. There is a strong satire, in
the first scene, on men whose lives have been spent
uselessly to society—

> "Formal beards,
> Men, who have no other proof of their
> Long life, but that they are old ! "

Villanor's idea in the first scene of the fourth act
has been copied by Moore in his earlier poems—

> " Look babies again in our eyes."

Brennoralt's reflections on the king's gifts and
honours are touchingly expressed—

> " A princely gift, but, sir, it comes too late !
> Like sunbeams on the blasted blossoms do
> Your favours fall."

Suckling has not scrupled to introduce without
any acknowledgment several entire lines of Shakespeare, and is also convicted of having borrowed
largely from " Balzac's Letters." [1]   " Brennoralt "
was first published under the title of the " Discontented Colonel," as a satire on the Scottish malcontents.

[1] In the " Epistolæ Hoelianæ " (edit. 1754, pp. 1, 211)
are two letters from Howell, in 1627 and 1628 respectively,
to Sir J. S., Knight, which were perhaps addressed to
Suckling. The two pieces of evidence of this are the passage in the first, where he returns to his correspondent
Suckling's favourite " Balzac," and in the second, where
he refers to his friend's " Harwich Neighbours." Among
Howell's correspondents was a Sir John Smith, whose
initials, of course, would be the same.]

Suckling has also appeared before us on two occasions as a translator; and notwithstanding the just objections of Dr. Johnson[1] to the style of literal translation pursued during the early part of the seventeenth century, Sir John's version of the little French ode beginning—

> " A quoy servent d'artifices,"

forms a marked and happy exception to the general usage. It unites much freedom and grace with very great fidelity to the original, and leaves us to regret that more of the light ballads and odes of our neighbours had not engaged his attention.

Suckling's works[2] have gone through many editions, but are, notwithstanding, rather scarce at the present day. The following will, I believe, be found a correct list of the successive republications of his writings :—

1. FRAGMENTA AUREA.—A collection of all the incomparable Peeces written by Sir John Suckling; and published by a friend to perpetuate his memory. Printed by his own copies. London : Printed for Humphrey Moseley, &c., 1646, 8º. It contains his Poems and Letters, and "An Account of Religion by Reason," with a portrait by W. Marshall.[3]

2. FRAGMENTA AUREA, &c. London : Printed for Humphrey Moseley, &c., 1648, 8º. The contents are the same as in the previous edition, and it has [the same portrait.]

---

[1] *Idler*, No. 69.

[2] [Besides the editions of the works of Suckling, nearly all the printed and manuscript miscellanies of the seventeenth century contain some of his pieces. His " Ballad of a Wedding " appeared during his lifetime in *Witt's Recreations*, 1640.]

[3] [With some anonymous lines beneath it. They were, however, the composition of Thomas Stanley. See "Stanley's Poems," 1651, p. 77.]

3. [FRAGMENTA AUREA, &c. The Third Edition, with
some New Additionals. London : Printed for Humphrey Moseley, &c., 1658, 8º, with the same portrait.

 .˙. The *Additionals* have a separate title, dated 1659.
They consist of supplementary poems and letters, and
the tragedy of "The Sad One," not before printed.]¹

4. [THE WORKS OF SIR JOHN SUCKLING. Con-
taining all his Poems, &c. London : Printed for, &c.
&c., 1696, 8º, with separate titles, dated 1694. Portrait, without the engraver's name, after Marshall.]

5. THE WORKS OF SIR JOHN SUCKLING. Con-
taining his Poems, Letters, and Plays. London :
Printed for Jacob Tonson, 1709, 8º, with a portrait.

6. THE WORKS OF SIR JOHN SUCKLING. Con-
taining his Poems, Letters and Plays. London :
Printed for Jacob Tonson, at Shakespeare's Head,
over against Katharine Street, in the Strand, 1719,
8º, with a portrait.

7. THE WORKS OF SIR JOHN SUCKLING. Con-
taining his Poems, Letters, and Plays. No portrait
is prefixed. 2 vols., 12º, 1770.

---

¹ [In this third impression the new matter is introduced
by a separate title, as follows :—"The Last Remains of
Sir John Suckling. Being a Full Collection of all his
Poems and Letters, which have been so long expected,
and never till now published, with the licence and appro-
bation of his noble and dearest friends." This impression
is undoubtedly of importance and value, and is compa-
ratively unknown. In the "Ballad on a Wedding," it
supplies an additional stanza, and the new matter at the
end, furnished (as we are told) by lady Southcot. more
than doubles the number of poems, as found in the octavos
of 1646 and 1648. So far as the volume, however, merely
reproduces the old matter, its text is decidedly inferior.
Of the edition of 1658 there is a reissue, perhaps a sur-
reptitious one, with the same title, imprint and date, but
with different typographical ornaments, and altogether a
distinct setting-up. It is accompanied by a portrait, copied
from Marshall's, and without any engraver's name.]

A LIST OF THE ENGRAVED PORTRAITS
OF SIR JOHN SUCKLING.

1. A bust, engraved by Cross; painter unknown.
2. A portrait prefixed to his "Poems and Plays," 1646, 8º. Painter uncertain; engraved by Marshall.
3. A portrait prefixed to the edition of his works, 1709, 8º. Painted by Vandyke; engraved by Vander Gucht.
4. A second engraving by Vander Gucht, from a portrait formerly in the possession of the family. [Probably the portrait before the edition of 1696 is here meant.]
5. A portrait of the poet as a child, with ruffles at the wrists.
6. A portrait, large folio, in the set of "Poets." Painted by Vandyke; engraved by Vertue, 1741.
7. A portrait prefixed to the selection from the works, 1836. Painted by Vandyke; engraved by James Thomson, 1835.
8. [A portrait taken in early life, half-length, the hair flowing. Engraved by Newton from a drawing by Thurston, after an original picture in the Ashmolean Museum at Oxford. In the series of "Portraits of the British Poets."]
9. [The anonymous print prefixed to the spurious edition of 1658 already referred to.]

TO THE MOST HONOURED AND HIGHLY DESERVING THE LADY SOUTHCOT.

THOUGH I approach with all humility in presenting these poems to your ladyship, yet dare I not despair of their acceptation, since it were a kind of felony to offer them to any other. They come to you at so many capacities, that they seem rather to return and rebound back to you, as the famous Arcadia was sent to that excellent lady who was sister to that great author. Your ladyship best knows that I now bring the last remains of your memorable brother, Sir John Suckling. And as here are all the world will ever hope for, so here are nothing else but his, not a line but what at first flowed from him—and will soon approve itself to be too much his to be altered or supplied by any other hand; and sure he were a bold man had thoughts to attempt it. After which 'twould be high presumption in me to say more, but that I am, madam, your ladyship's most obliged and most obedient humble servant,

HUM. MOSELEY.[1]

[1] First printed in the edition of 1658. Respecting Lady Southcot, see Memoir.

THE STATIONER TO THE READER.[1]

AMONG the highest and most refined wits of the
nation, this gentle and princely poet took
his generous rise from the Court, where, having
flourished with splendour and reputation, he lived
only long enough to see the sunset of that majesty
from whose auspicious beams he derived his lustre,
and with whose declining state his own loyal fortunes were obscured. But after the several changes
of those times, being sequestered from the more
serene contentments of his native country, he first
took care to secure the dearest and choicest of his
papers in the several cabinets of his noble and
faithful friends, and among other testimonies of
his worth, these elegant and florid pieces of his
fancy were preserved in the custody of his truly
honourable and virtuous sister, with whose free per-
mission they were transcribed, and now published
exactly according to the originals.

This might be suffcient to make you acknowledge that these are the real and genuine works of
Sir John Suckling; but if you can yet doubt, let
any judicious soul seriously consider the freedom
of the fancy, richness of the conceipt, proper expression, with that air and spirit diffused through
every part, and he will find such a perfect resemblance with what hath been formerly known, that
he cannot with modesty doubt them to be his.

[1] [This preface is common to the editions of 1646, '48,
'58.]

I could tell you further (for I myself am the best witness of it), that a thirst and general inquiry hath been after what I here present you, by all that have either seen or heard of them. And by that time you have read them, you will believe me, who have, now for many years, annually published the productions of the best wits of our own and foreign nations.

H. M.

TO THE READER.[1]

WHILE Suckling's name is in the forehead of this book, these poems can want no preparation. It had been a prejudice to posterity they should have slept longer, and an injury to his own ashes. They that conversed with him alive and truly, under which notion I comprehend only knowing gentlemen, his soul (being transcendent and incommunicable to others but by reflection), will honour these posthumous Ideas of their friend; and if any have lived in so much darkness as not to have known so great an ornament to our age, by looking upon these Remains with civility and understanding, they may timely yet repent and be forgiven.

In this age of paper-prostitution a man may buy the price of some authors into the price of their volume; but know, the name that leadeth into this Elysium is sacred to Art and Honour, and no man that is not excellent in both is qualified a competent judge. For when knowledge is allowed, yet education in the course of a gentleman requires as many descents as go to make one, and he that is bold upon his unequal stock to traduce this Name, or learning, will deserve to be condemned again into ignorance (his original sin), and die in it.

But I keep back the ingenuous reader by my unworthy preface. The gate is open, and thy soul

[1] This notice precedes the "Last Remains" in the edition of 1658. Not in editions of 1646, '48.

invited to a garden of ravishing variety. Admire
his wit that created these for thy delight, while I
withdraw into a shade, and contemplate who must
follow.[1]

[1] [This preface, though unsigned, was almost certainly
written by Humphrey Moseley, the stationer. In the last
sentence he refers, of course, to the next poet to be undertaken, as a sequel to Suckling.]

POEMS.

A

[SEPARATE TITLE TO THE POEMS, 1646-8-58.[1]]

Poems, &c., written by Sir John Suckling. Printed by his owne copy. The Lyrick Poems were set in Musick by Mr. Henry Lawes, Gent., of the Kings Chappell, and one of His Majesties Private Musick.

A chronological or other systematic arrangement of Suckling's lyric and miscellaneous pieces should have been attempted; but, on examination, the process appeared to be one of peculiar difficulty, without being, on the whole, perhaps, of very great importance. The chief part have no note of time.

---

[1] The variations are only orthographical.

POEMS.

ON NEW-YEAR'S DAY, 1640. TO THE KING.

1.

AWAKE, great sir, the sun shines here,
    Gives all your subjects a New-Year,
  Only we stay till you appear ;
For thus by us your power is understood ;
He may make fair days, you must make them good.
      Awake, awake,
        And take
Such presents as poor men can make,
They can add little unto bliss
    Who cannot wish.

2.

  May no ill vapour cloud the sky,
  Bold storms invade the sovereignty,
  But gales of joy, so fresh, so high,
That you may think Heaven sent to try this year
What sail, or burthen, a king's mind could bear.
      Awake, awake, &c.

3.

May all the discords in your state
(Like those in music we create),
Be governed at so wise a rate,

That what would of itself sound harsh, or fright,
May be so tempered that it may delight.
    Awake, awake, &c.

4.

What conquerors from battles find,
Or lovers when their doves are kind,
Take up henceforth our master's mind,
Make such strange rapes upon the place, 't may be—
No longer joy there, but an ecstasy.
    Awake, awake, &c.

5.

May every pleasure and delight,
That has, or does, your sense invite,
Double this year, save those o' th' night ;
   Awake, awake,
   And take
Such presents as poor men can make,
They can add little unto bliss
  Who cannot wish.

LOVING AND BELOVED.

1.

THERE never yet was honest man
  That ever drove the trade of love ;
It is impossible, nor can
  Integrity our ends promove ;
For kings and lovers are alike in this,
That their chief art in reign dissembling is.

2.

Here we are loved, and there we love :
  Good nature now and passion strive
Which of the two should be above,
  And laws unto the other give.

So we false fire with art sometimes discover,
And the true fire with the same art do cover.

3.

What rack can fancy find so high ?
Here we must court, and here engage ;
Though in the other place we die.
O, 'tis torture all, and cosenage !
And which the harder is I cannot tell,
To hide true love, or make false love look well.

4.

Since it is thus, god of desire,
Give me my honesty again,
And take thy brands back, and thy fire ;
I am weary of the state I am in :
Since (if the very best should now befall),
Love's triumph must be Honour's funeral.

1.

IF when Don Cupid's dart[1]
Doth wound a heart,
We hide our grief
And shun relief ;
The smart increaseth on that score ;
For wounds unsearched but rankle more.

2.

Then if we whine, look pale,
And tell our tale,
Men are in pain
For us again ;

[1] "Rochester and others among the early poets have written poems on the model of this, and Leigh Hunt among the moderns."—*W. W.*

So neither speaking doth become
The lover's state, nor being dumb.

3.

When this I do descry,
Then thus think I :
    Love is the fart
    Of every heart ;
It pains a man when 'tis kept close,
And others doth offend when 'tis let loose.

A Session of the Poets.

A SESSION was held the other day,
    And Apollo himself was at it, they say,
The laurel that had been so long reserved,
Was now to be given to him best deserved.

    And

Therefore the wits of the town came thither,
'Twas strange to see how they flocked together,
Each strongly confident of his own [s]way,
Thought to gain the laurel away that day.

    And

There was Selden, and he sat hard by the chair ;
Wenman[1] not far off, which was very fair ;
Sands[2] with Townsend,[3] for they kept no order ;
Digby[4] and Shillingsworth[5] a little further.

    And

[1] No poet of this name is known, unless it was Thomas Wenman, author of the "Legend of Mary, Queen of Scots," printed by Fry, from an MS., in 1810.

[2] George Sandys.   [3] Aurelian Townshend.

[4] This could hardly be George Digby, Earl of Bristol. He must have been a very young man in 1637, the reputed date of the composition of this poem.

[5] Chillingworth, the divine, cannot here be intended, as supposed by Mr. Suckling ("Selections," 1856, p. 86).

There was Lucan's translator, too,[1] and he
That makes God speak so big in 's poetry ;[2]
Selwin and Waller,[3] and Bartlets[4] both the brothers ;
Jack Vaughan[5] and Porter,[6] and divers others.

The first that broke silence was good old Ben,
Prepared before with canary wine,
And he told them plainly he deserved the bays,
For his were called works, where others were but
  plays.

And

Bid them remember how he had purged the stage
Of errors, that had lasted many an age ;
And he hoped they did not think the "Silent
  Woman,"
The "Fox," and the "Alchemist," outdone by no
  man.

Apollo stopped him there, and bade him not go on,
'Twas merit, he said, and not presumption,
Must carry 't ; at which Ben turned about,
And in great choler offered to go out.

But

Those that were there thought it not fit
To discontent so ancient a wit ;
And therefore Apollo called him back again,
And made him mine host of his own New Inn.

---

[1] Thomas May.   [2] Query, Francis Quarles.
[3] The copy of 1658 has *Walter*.
[4] I know nothing decidedly of the writings of these
brothers. There was a William Bartlett, who published,
in 1647 and 1649, two quarto volumes on religious subjects;
but I doubt if he be the same author to whom Suckling
alludes.—*Note in edit.* 1836.
[5] Sir John Vaughan. He was a secret enemy to monarchy, though he never engaged in any open hostility
against Charles the First. He died in 1674, and was
buried in the Temple Church by his friend Selden, to
whose will he had acted as executor.—*Note in edit.* 1836.
[6] Endymion Porter.

Tom Carew[1] was next, but he had fault
That would not well stand with a laureat ;
His muse was hide-bound,[2] and the issue of 's brain
Was seldom brought forth but with trouble and pain.

                                              And

All that were present there did agree,
A laureate muse should be easy and free,
Yet sure 'twas not that, but 'twas thought that, his
    grace
Considered, he was well he had a cup-bearer's place.

Will. Davenant, ashamed of a foolish mischance,
That he had got lately travelling in France,
Modestly hoped the handsomeness of 's muse
Might any deformity about him excuse.

                                              And

Surely the company would have been content,
If they could have found any precedent ;
But in all their records either in verse or prose,
There was not one laureate without a nose.

To Will. Bartlett sure all the wits meant well,
But first they would see how his snow would sell :
Will. smiled and swore in their judgments they
    went less,
That concluded of merit upon success.

Suddenly taking his place again,
He gave way to Selwin, who straight stepped in,
But, alas ! he had been so lately a wit,
That Apollo hardly knew him yet.

[1] "Carew's poems have been lately reprinted, and have
not obtained much notice. He is chiefly known as the
author of the beautiful sonnet beginning 'He that a coral
lip admires.'"—*W. W.* The "sonnet" referred to is the
copy of verses entitled *Disdain Returned* (Hazlitt's edit.,
1870, p. 21).
[2] So. edit. 1648 ; edits. 1646 and 1658 read *hard-bound.*

Toby Matthews[1] (pox on him!), how came he there?
Was whispering nothing in somebody's ear;
When he had the honour to be named in court,
But, sir, you may thank my Lady Carlisle for 't:

For had not her care furnished you out
With something of handsome, without all doubt
You and your sorry Lady Muse had been
In the number of those that were not let in.

In haste from the court two or three came in,
And they brought letters, forsooth, from the Queen;
'Twas discreetly done, too, for if th' had come
Without them, th' had scarce been let into the room.

Suckling next was called, but did not appear,
But straight one whispered Apollo i' th' ear,
That of all men living he cared not for 't,
He loved not the Muses so well as his sport.

And prized black eyes, or a lucky hit
At bowls, above all the trophies of wit;
But Apollo was angry, and publicly said,
'Twere fit that a fine were set upon 's head.

Wat Montague[2] now stood forth to his trial,
And did not so much as suspect a denial;

[1] Toby Matthews. The reader will find a long notice of this eccentric character in Walpole's "Anecdotes of Painting." His Lordship calls him "one of those heteroclite animals who finds his place anywhere. His father was Archbishop of York, and he a Jesuit. He was supposed a wit, and believed himself a politician: his works are ridiculous." Suckling has introduced him in the same manner as he has "Jack Bond" and Tom Carew, as an occasional interlocutor with himself in his poems. His "whispering nothing in somebody's ear" alludes to a ridiculous habit he had of whispering in company.—*Note in edit.* 1836.

[2] The Honourable Walter Montague, author of "Miscellanea Spiritualia," 1648.

"Wat Montague wrote the 'Shepherd's Paradise,' pub-

But witty Apollo asked him first of all,
If he understood his own pastoral.

For, if he could do it, 'twould plainly appear,
He understood more than any man there,
And did merit the bays above all the rest,
But the Monsieur was modest, and silence confessed.

During these troubles, in the crowd was hid
One that Apollo soon missed, little Cid;[1]
And having spied him call'd him out of the throng,
And advis'd him in his ear not to write so strong.

Then Murray[2] was summon'd, but 'twas urged
    that he
Was chief already of another company.

Hales[3] set by himself most gravely did smile
To see them about nothing keep such a coil;
Apollo had spied him, but knowing his mind
Passed by, and call'd Falkland that sat just behind.

                                   But

He was of late so gone with divinity,
That he had almost forgot his poetry;
Though to say the truth (and Apollo did know it)
He might have been both his priest and his poet.

lished in 1659, 8vo. He was a papist, and suspected of
having been concerned in the conversion of Lady New-
burgh. On that occasion, it is said in a letter of Lord
Conway's, 'The king did use such words of Wat Montagu
and Sir Tobie Matthew, that the fright made Wat keep
his chamber longer than his sickness would have detained
him.'"—*Note in edit.* 1836.

[1] Probably Joseph Rutter, author of an English version
of Corneille's *Cid*, 1637-40.

[2] William Murray.

[3] Query, Sir Matthew Hale, who seems to have been on
terms of intimacy with many of the wits of the day. Or,
as Mr. Suckling supposed, it may refer to John Hales of
Eton, the known friend of Carew, to whom Suckling elsewhere addresses an epistle.

At length who but an Alderman did appear,
At which Will. Davenant began to swear;
But wiser Apollo bade him draw nigher,
And when he was mounted a little higher,

He openly declared that it was the best sign
Of good store of wit to have good store of coin;
And without a syllable more or less said
He put the laurel on the Alderman's head.

At this all the wits were in such amaze
That for a good while they did nothing but gaze
One upon another: not a man in the place
But had discontent writ in great in his face.

Only the small poets cheer'd up again,
Out of hope, as 'twas thought, of borrowing;
But sure they were out, for he forfeits his crown,
When he lends to any poet about the town.[1]

LOVE'S WORLD.[2]

IN each man's heart that doth begin
    To love, there's ever framed within
A little world, for so I found
When first my passion reason drown'd.

Instead of earth unto this frame,   *Earth.*
I had a faith was still the same;

---

[1] " The characters of the poets who appeal at the Sessions
are drawn with great discrimination, particularly that of
the poet Jonson.   His own attachment to pleasure and indifference to fame are expressed with great [word illegible
in MS.].   Some poems on the model of this will be found
in the 'State Poems;' but they all appear to me inferior
in grace and simplicity."—*W. W.*

[2] " This ode abounds with the most childish conceits, but
which are occasionally redeemed by beauties of the highest
order.   Byron apparently imitated the last two lines of the
fourth stanza. . . . Some of the thoughts [in the latter part]
are somewhat free, though quaintly expressed."—*W. W.*

For to be right it doth behove
It be as that, fixed and not move.

Yet as the earth may sometimes shake
(For winds shut up will cause a quake),
So often jealousy and fear,
Stolen into mine, cause tremblings there.

My Flora was my sun, for as   *Sun.*
One sun, so but one Flora, was;
All other faces borrowed hence
Their light and grace, as stars do thence.

My hopes I call my moon, for they   *Moon.*
Inconstant still were at no stay;
But as my sun inclined to me,
Or more or less were sure to be.

Sometimes it would be full, and then
O, too—too soon decrease again;
Eclipsed sometimes that 'twould so fall
There would appear no hope at all.

My thoughts, 'cause infinite they be,   *Stars.*
Must be those many stars we see;
Of which some wandered at their will,   *Fixed*
But most on her were fixed still.   *Planets.*

My burning flame and hot desire   *Elements*
Must be the element of fire,   *of fire.*
Which hath as yet no secret been,
That it as that was never seen.

No kitchen fire nor eating flame,
But innocent: hot but in name;
A fire that's starved when fed, and gone
When too much fuel is laid on.

But as it plainly doth appear
That fire subsists by being near

The moon's bright orb, so I believe
Ours doth, for hope keeps love alive.

My fancy[1] was the air, most free   *Air.*
And full of mutability ;
Big with chimeras, vapours here
Innumerable hatched as there.

The sea's my mind, which calm would be   *Sea.*
Were it from winds (my passions) free ;
But out, alas ! no sea I find
Is troubled like a lover's mind.

Within it rocks and shallows be :
Despair and fond credulity.

But in this world it were good reason
We did distinguish time and season ;
Her presence then did make the day,
And night shall come when she's away.

Long absence in far-distant place   *Winter.*
Creates the winter ; and the space
She tarried with me, well I might
Call it my summer of delight.   *Summer.*

Diversity of weather came
From what she did, and thence had name ;
Sometimes sh' would smile—that made it fair ;
And when she laughed, the sun shined clear.

Sometimes sh' would frown, and sometimes weep,
So clouds and rain their turns do keep ;
Sometimes again sh' would be all ice,
Extremely cold, extremely nice.

---

[1] "Scott, in his *Life of Byron*, has quoted these two lines."—*W. W.*

But soft, my muse, the world is wide,
And all at once was not descried :
It may fall out some honest lover
The rest hereafter will discover.

SONNETS.[1]

1.

DOST see how unregarded now
  That piece of beauty passes ?
There was a time when I did vow
   To that alone ;
  But mark the fate of faces ;
The red and white works now no more on me,
Than if it could not charm, or I not see.

2.

And yet the face continues good,
  And I have still desires,
And still the self-same flesh and blood,
   As apt to melt,
  And suffer from those fires ;
O, some kind power unriddle where it lies :
Whether my heart be faulty, or her eyes ?

3.

She every day her man does kill,
  And I as often die ;
Neither her power then nor my will
   Can questioned be ;
  What is the mystery ?
Sure beauty's empires, like to greater states,
Have certain periods set, and hidden fates.

---

[1] In the old copies, the familiar song beginning "Why so pale" precedes these sonnets ; but it is evidently an erroneous repetition, as it is given again *in extenso* in its proper place, the fourth act of "Aglaura."

II.

1.

OF thee, kind boy, I ask no red and white,
  To make up my delight:
   No odd becoming graces,
Black eyes, or little know-not-whats in faces;
Make me but mad enough, give me good store
Of love for her I court:
  I ask no more,
'Tis love in love that makes the sport.

2.

There's no such thing as that we beauty call,
  It is mere cosenage all;
   For though some long ago
Like t' certain colours mingled so and so,
That doth not tie me now from choosing new.
If I a fancy take
  To black and blue,
That fancy doth it beauty make.

3.

'Tis not the meat, but 'tis the appetite
  Makes eating a delight,
   And if I like one dish
More than another, that a pheasant is;
What in our watches, that in us is found;
So to the height and nick
  We up be wound,
No matter by what hand or trick.

III.

1.

O FOR some honest lover's ghost,[1]
  Some kind unbodied post
  Sent from the shades below !
  I strangely long to know,
Whether the nobler chaplets wear,
Those that their mistress' scorn did bear,
   Or those that were used kindly.

2.

For whatsoe'er they tell us here
  To make those sufferings dear,
  'Twill there I fear be found,
  That to the being crowned
T' have loved alone will not suffice,
Unless we also have been wise,
   And have our loves enjoyed.

3.

What posture can we think him in,
  That here unloved again
  Departs, and 's thither gone,
  Where each sits by his own ?
Or how can that elysium be,
Where I my mistress still must see
   Circled in others' arms ?

4.

For there the judges all are just,
  And Sophonisba must

[1] "Many poets have expressed the same wish. See James Greene's ' Girls' Dreams.' "—*Anon.*

Be his whom she held dear,
Not his who loved her here.
The sweet Philoclea, since she died,
Lies by her Pirocles his side,
Not by Amphialus.

5.

Some bays, perchance, or myrtle bough,
For difference crowns the brow
Of those kind souls that were
The noble martyrs here ;
And if that be the only odds,
(As who can tell?) ye kinder gods,
Give me the woman here.

To HIS MUCH HONOURED THE LORD LEPINGTON, UPON HIS TRANSLATION OF MALVEZZI, HIS "ROMULUS" AND "TARQUIN."[1]

IT is so rare and new a thing to see
Ought that belongs to young nobility[2]
In print, but their own clothes, that we must praise
You as we would do those first show the ways
To arts or to new worlds. , You have begun ;
Taught travelled youth what 'tis it should have done
For 't has indeed too strong a custom been
To carry out more wit than we bring in.
You have done otherwise : brought home, my lord,
The choicest things famed countries do afford :
Malvezzi by your means is English grown,
And speaks our tongue as well now as his own.

[1] This book by Henry Cary, Lord Lepington, was printed in 1637.
[2] "This reminds us of Byron :—

'And 'tis some praise in peers to write at all.'

Malvezzi's work is now rather rare, at least in the translation."—*W. W.*

Malvezzi, he whom 'tis as hard to praise
To merit, as to imitate his ways.
He does not show us Rome great suddenly,
As if the empire were a tympany,
But gives it natural growth, tells how and why
The little body grew so large and high.
Describes each thing so lively that we are
Concerned ourselves before we are aware :
And at the wars they and their neighbours waged,
Each man is present still, and still engaged.
Like a good prospective he strangely brings
Things distant to us ; and in these two kings
We see what made greatness.   And what 't has been
Made that greatness contemptible again.
And all this not tediously derived,
But like to worlds in little maps contrived.
'Tis he that doth the Roman dame restore,
Makes Lucrece chaster for her being whore ;
Gives her a kind revenge for Tarquin's sin ;
For ravish'd first, she ravisheth again.
She says such fine things after 't, that we must
In spite of virtue thank foul rape and lust,
Since 'twas the cause no woman would have had,
Though she's of Lucrece side, Tarquin less bad.
But stay ; like one that thinks to bring his friend
A mile or two, and sees the journey's end,
I strangle on too far ; long graces do
But keep good stomachs off, that would fall to.

Against Fruition.

STAY here, fond youth, and ask no more, be wise :
    Knowing too much long since lost paradise.
The virtuous joys thou hast, thou wouldst should
    still
Last in their pride ; and wouldst not take it ill,
If rudely from sweet dreams (and for a toy)
Thou wert wak't ? he wakes himself, that does enjoy.

Fruition adds no new wealth, but destroys,
And while it pleaseth much the palate, cloys ;
Who thinks he shall be happier for that,
As reasonably might hope he might grow fat
By eating to a surfeit ; this once pass'd,
What relishes ? even kisses lose their taste.

Urge not 'tis necessary, alas ! we know
The homeliest thing which mankind does is so ;
The world is of a vast extent, we see,
And must be peopled ; children there must be ;
So must bread too ; but since they are enough
Born to the drudgery, what need we plough ?

Women enjoyed (whate'er before t' have been)
Are like romances read, or sights once seen ;
Fruition's dull, and spoils the play much more,
Than if one read or knew the plot before ;
'Tis expectation makes a blessing dear,
Heaven were not heaven, if we knew what it were.

And as in prospects we are there pleased most,
Where something keeps the eye from being lost,
And leaves us room to guess : so here restraint
Holds up delight, that with excess would faint.
They who know all the wealth they have, are poor,
He's only rich that cannot tell his store.

1.

THERE never yet was woman made,[1]
    Nor shall, but to be cursed,
And O, that I, fond I, should first,
    Of any lover,
This truth at my own charge to other fools discover !

[1] "This poem is remarkable for ease and sprightliness,
the true characteristics of Sir J. Suckling's verse, and
may therefore be taken as a fair specimen of his powers.
Suckling seems to have been intimately acquainted with

2.

You that have promised to yourselves
    Propriety in love,   ·
Know women's hearts like straw do move;
    And what we call
Their sympathy, is but love to jet in general.

3.

All mankind are alike to them;
    And though we iron find
That never with a loadstone joined,
    'Tis not the iron's fault,
It is because near the loadstone yet it was never
    brought.

4.

If where a gentle bee hath fallen,
    And laboured to his power,
A new succeeds not to that flower,
    But passes by,
'Tis to be thought, the gallant elsewhere loads his
    thigh.

5.

For still the flowers ready stand,
    One buzzes round about,
One lights, one tastes, gets in, gets out;
    All always use them,
Till all their sweets are gone, and all again refuse
    them.[1]

the female heart; he praises, ridicules, and adores the sex in the same breath. The germs of thought in some of Moore's most beautiful lyrics may be found in this ode."
— *W. W.*

[1] In the old copies the song, " No, no, fair heretic," &c., follows here; but see it in the fourth act of " Aglaura."

To my Friend Will. Davenant, upon his Poem of "Madagascar."[1]

WHAT mighty princes poets are ? those things
    The great ones stick at, and our very kings
Lay down, they venture on ; and with great ease
Discover, conquer what and where they please.
Some phlegmatic sea-captain would have stay'd
For money now, or victuals ; not have weighed
Anchor without 'em ; thou (Will.) dost not stay
So much as for a wind, but goest away,
Land'st, view'st, the country ; fight'st, puts all to
    rout,
Before another could be putting out !
And now the news in town is—Davenant's come
From Madagascar, fraught with laurel home ;
And welcome, Will., for the first time ; but prithee,
In thy next voyage bring the gold too with thee.

To my Friend Will. Davenant, on his other Poems.

THOU hast redeemed us, Will., and future times
    Shall not account unto the age's crimes
Dearth of pure wit : since the great lord of it
(Donne) parted hence, no man has ever writ
So near him in 's own way ; I would commend
Particulars ; but then, how should I end
Without a volume ? every line of thine
Would ask (to praise it right) twenty of mine.

[1] This, as well as the following copy of verses, was prefixed to Davenant's poems, 1638. Several poems addressed
to Davenant will be found in the present volume.

1.

LOVE, Reason, Hate, did once bespeak
    Three mates to play at barley-break ;
Love Folly took ; and Reason Fancy ;
And Hate consorts with Pride ; so dance they.
Love coupled last, and so it fell,
That Love and Folly were in hell.

2.

They break, and Love would Reason meet,
But Hate was nimbler on her feet ;
Fancy looks for Pride, and thither
Hies, and they two hug together :
Yet this new coupling still doth tell,
That Love and Folly were in hell.

3.

The rest do break again, and Pride
Hath now got Reason on her side ;
Hate and Fancy meet, and stand
Untouched by Love in Folly's hand ;
Folly was dull, but love ran well :
So Love and Folly were in hell.

Song.

1.

I PRITHEE spare me, gentle boy,[1]
    Press me no more for that slight toy,
That foolish trifle of an heart ;
I swear it will not do its part,
Though thou dost thine, employ'st thy power and art.

---

[1] "Moore has borrowed the idea of some of his best
. . . from this ode."—*W. W.* Below the fourth stanza he
notes: "This is not only poetical, but too fine [?fine too]."

2.

For through long custom it has known
The little secrets, and is grown
Sullen and wise, will have its will,'
And, like old hawks, pursues that still
That makes least sport, flies only where 't can kill.

3.

Some youth that has not made his story,
Will think, perchance, the pain's the glory;
And mannerly fit out love's feast;
I shall be carving of the best,
Rudely call for the last course 'fore the rest.

4.

And, O, when once that course is pass'd,
How short a time the feast doth last!
Men rise away, and scarce say grace,
Or civilly once thank the face
That did invite, but seek another place.

UPON MY LADY CARLISLE'S WALKING IN HAMPTON COURT GARDEN.[1]

Dialogue.

T[HOMAS] C[AREW].   J[OHN] S[UCKLING].

TOM.

DIDST thou not find the place inspired,
    And flowers, as if they had desired

---

[1] "Excellence in poetry was not understood in that age. Obscurity was mistaken for sublimity, and pedantry for learning. Nature and simplicity were banished from poetry. Milton and Dryden alone seem to have under-

No other sun, start from their beds,
And for a sight steal out their heads?
Heard'st thou not music when she talked
And didst not find that as she walked
She threw rare perfumes all about,
Such as bean-blossoms newly out,
Or chafed spices give?——

J. S.

I must confess those perfumes, Tom,
I did not smell; nor found that from
Her passing by ought sprang up new;
The flowers had all their birth from you;
For I passed over the self-same walk,
And did not find one single stalk
Of anything that was to bring
This unknown after-after-spring.

TOM.

Dull and insensible, couldst see
A thing so near a Deity
Move up and down, and feel no change?

J. S.

None and so great were alike strange,
I had my thoughts, but not your way;
All are not born, sir, to the bay;

stood the true principles of poetry, and were not vitiated
by the prevailing taste. Milton, for the sake of temporary
celebrity, would not conform to the reigning taste, and
was therefore not popular. . . . . Carew was a courtier,
and in some fame with Charles I., who conferred several
honourable offices on him. Some of his lyrical poems are
very beautiful, though occasionally deformed by obscuri-
ties. He, like his friend Suckling, was ambitious of being
ranked among the metaphysical poets, but fortunately had
not power to attain it."—*W. W.* It may be just added
that the Lady Carlisle here named can hardly have been
any other than the wife of James Hay, first Earl of that
creation, 1622-36.

Alas! Tom, I am flesh and blood,
And was consulting how I could
In spite of masks and hoods descry
The parts denied unto the eye;
I was undoing all she wore,
And had she walked but one turn more,
Eve in her first state had not been
More naked, or more plainly seen.

TOM.

'Twas well for thee she left the place,
There is great danger in that face;
But hadst thou viewed her leg and thigh
And upon that discovery
Searched after parts that are more dear
(As fancy seldom stops so near),
No time or age had ever seen
So lost a thing as thou hadst been.

To Mr. Davenant for Absence.

WONDER not, if I stay not here,
    Hurt lovers, like to wounded deer,
Must shift the place; for standing still
Leaves too much time to know our ill:
Where there is a traitor eye,
That lets in from th' enemy
All that may supplant an heart,
'Tis time the chief should use some art.
Who parts the object from the sense,
Wisely cuts off intelligence.
O, how quickly men must die,
Should they stand all love's battery!
Persinda's eyes great mischief do,
So do we know the cannon too;
But men are safe at distance still:

Where they reach not, they cannot kill.
Love is a fit, and soon is pass'd,
Ill diet only makes it last;
Who is still looking, gazing ever,
Drinks wine i' th' very height o' th' fever.

AGAINST ABSENCE.

MY whining lover, what needs all
   These vows of life monastical?
Despairs, retirements, jealousies,
And subtle sealing up of eyes?
Come, come, be wise; return again,
A finger burnt 's as great a pain;
And the same physic, self-same art
Cures that, would cure a flaming heart,
Wouldst thou, whilst yet the fire is in it,
But hold it to the fire again?
If you, dear sir, the plague have got,
What matter is 't whether or not
They let you in the same house lie,
Or carry you abroad to die?
He whom the plague or love once takes,
Every room a pest-house makes.
Absence were good if 'twere but sense,
That only holds th' intelligence:
Pure love alone no hurt would do,
But love is love and magic too;
Brings a mistress a thousand miles,
And the sleight of looks beguiles,
Makes her entertain thee there,
And the same time your rival here;
And (O the devil) that she should
Say finer things now than she would;
So nobly fancy doth supply
What the dull sense lets fall and die.
Beauty, like man's old enemy, is known

To tempt him most when he's alone :
The air of some wild o'ergrown wood
Or pathless grove is the boy's food.
Return then back, and feed thine eye,
Feed all thy senses, and feast high.
Spare diet is the cause love lasts,
For surfeits sooner kill than fasts.

A Supplement[1] of an Imperfect Copy of Verses of Mr. William Shakespeare's, by the Author.

1.

ONE of her hands one of her cheeks lay under,
  Cosening the pillow of a lawful kiss,
Which therefore swelled, and seemed to part asunder,
  As angry to be robbed of such a bliss !
    The one looked pale and for revenge did long,
    While t' other blushed, 'cause it had done the wrong.

2.

Out of the bed the other fair hand was
  On a green satin quilt, whose perfect white
Looked like a daisy in a field of grass,
  And showed like unmelt snow unto the sight ;
    There lay this pretty perdue, safe to keep
    The rest o' th' body that lay fast asleep.

3.

Her eyes (and therefore it was night), close laid,
  Strove to imprison beauty till the morn :
But, yet the doors were of such fine stuff made,
  That it broke through, and showed itself in scorn,

---

[1] "The continuation is equal to the first part."—*W. W.*
[2] The allusion is to a well-known passage in "Lucrece."
[3] Thus far Shakespeare.

Throwing a kind of light about the place,
Which turned to smiles still, as 't came near
her face.

4.

Her beams, which some dull men called hair, divided,
Part with her cheeks, part with her lips did
sport.
But these, as rude, her breath put by still; some
Wiselier downwards sought, but falling short,
Curled back in rings, and seemed to turn
again
To bite the part so unkindly held them in.

THAT none beguiled be by time's quick flowing,
Lovers have in their hearts a clock still going;
For though time be nimble, his motions
Are quicker
And thicker
Where love hath his notions :

Hope is the mainspring on which moves desire,
And these do the less wheels, Fear, Joy, inspire ;
The balance is Thought, evermore
Clicking
And striking,
And ne'er giving o'er.

Occasion 's the hand which still 's moving round,
Till by it the critical hour may be found,
And when that falls out, it will strike
Kisses,
Strange blisses,
And what you best like.

1.

'TIS now since I sat down before
 That foolish fort, a heart,
(Time strangely spent) a year and more,
 And still I did my part:

2.

Made my approaches,[1] from her hand
 Unto her lip did rise,
And did already understand
 The language of her eyes.

3.

Proceeded on with no less art,
 My tongue was engineer;
I thought to undermine the heart
 By whispering in the ear.

4.

When this did nothing I brought down,
 Great cannon-oaths, and shot
A thousand thousand to the town,
 And still it yielded not.

5.

I then resolved to starve the place
 By cutting off all kisses,

[1] "Byron appears to have imitated this stanza in the following lines:—
 'Ours was the smile none saw beside;
 The glance that none might understand;
 The whisper'd thought of hearts allied;
 The pressure of the thrilling hand.'
In this poem Suckling seems to have succeeded completely in what is called the metaphysical style of poetry, which predominated in his time, and, like all the poetry of this school, is highly . . . but wants nature."—*W. W.*

Praying and gazing on her face,
    And all such little blisses.

6.

To draw her out, and from her strength
    I drew all batteries in :
And brought myself to lie at length,
    As if no siege had been.

7.

When I had done what man could do,
    And thought the place mine own,
The enemy lay quiet too,
    And smiled at all was done.

8.

I sent to know from whence and where
    These hopes and this relief ?
A spy informed, Honour was there,
    And did command in chief.

9.

March, march, quoth I, the word straight give,
    Let's lose no time, but leave her ;
That giant upon air will live,
    And hold it out for ever.

10.

To such a place our camp remove,
    As will no siege abide ;
I hate a fool that starves her love,
    Only to feed her pride.

UPON MY LORD BROHALL'S[1] WEDDING.

Dialogue.

S[UCKLING]. B[OND].[2]

S. IN bed, dull man,
　　When Love and Hymen's revels are begun
And the church ceremonies past and done !
B. Why, who 's gone mad to-day ?
S. Dull heretic, thou wouldest say,
　　He that is gone to heaven 's gone astray;
　　　　Brohall our gallant friend
Is gone to church, as martyrs to the fire :
　　Who marry, differ i' th' end,
　　　　Since both do take
The hardest way to what they most desire :
Nor stayed he till the formal priest had done,
But ere that part was finish'd, his begun :
　　　　Which did reveal
The haste and eagerness men have to seal,
　　　　That long to tell the money.
A sprig of willow in his hat he wore
(The loser's badge and liv'ry heretofore),
But now so ordered that it might be taken
By lookers-on, forsaking as forsaken.
　　　　And now and then
A careless smile broke forth, which spoke his mind,
And seem'd to say she might have been more kind.
　　When this (dear Jack) I saw,
　　　　　　Thought I,
　　How weak is lover's law ?
The bonds made there (like gipsies' knots) with ease
Are fast and loose, as·they that hold them please.

[1] [This poem was composed on the same occasion as the more celebrated " Ballad," the marriage of Suckling's friend, Roger Boyle, Lord Broghill.]
[2] [As to Jack Bond, see *Memoir.*]

B. But was the fair nymph's praise or power less
That led him captive now to happiness,
'Cause she did not a foreign aid despise,
But enter'd breaches made by others' eyes?
S.   The gods forbid!
There must be some to shoot and batter down,
Others to force and to take in the town.
          To hawks (good Jack) and harts
                              There may
          Be sev'ral ways and arts;
One watches them perchance, and makes them tame;
Another, when they are ready, shows them game.

SIR,[1]

W HETHER these lines do you find out,
          Putting or clearing of a doubt;
(Whether predestination,
Or reconciling three in one,
Or the unriddling how men die,
And live at once eternally,
Now take you up) know 'tis decreed
You straight bestride the college-steed:
Leave Socinus and the schoolmen
(Which Jack Bond swears do but fool men),
And come to town; 'tis fit you show
Yourself abroad, that men may know
(Whate'er some learned men have guess'd)
That oracles are not yet ceas'd:
There you shall find the wit and wine
Flowing alike, and both divine:
Dishes, with names not known in books,
And less amongst the college-cooks,
With sauce so pregnant that you need
Not stay till hunger bids you feed.

[1] This poetical epistle, which has considerable merit, is addressed by Suckling to his learned friend, John Hales of Eton: he was one of the first disciples of Socinus in this kingdom.—*Note in ed.* 1836.

The sweat of learned Johnson's brain,[1]
And gentle Shakespeare's eas'er strain,
A hackney-coach conveys you to,
In spite of all that rain can do:
And for your eighteenpence you sit
The lord and judge of all fresh wit.
News in one day as much w' have here,
As serves all Windsor for a year,
And which the carrier brings to you,
After 't has here been found not true.
Then think what company 's design'd
To meet you here, men so refin'd;
Their very common talk at board,
Makes wise or mad a young court-lord,
And makes him capable to be
Umpire in 's father's company.
Where no disputes nor forc'd defence
Of a man's person for his sense
Take up the time; all strive to be
Masters of truth, as victory:
And where you come, I'd boldly swear
A synod might as eas'ly err.

AGAINST FRUITION.

FIE upon hearts that burn with mutual fire:
  I hate two minds that breathe but one desire:
Were I to curse th' unhallow'd sort of men,
I'd wish them to love, and be lov'd again.
Love's a camelion, that lives on mere air;
And surfeits when it comes to grosser fare:
'Tis petty jealousies and little fears,

---

[1] "Compare Milton—

  'Then to the well-trod stage anon,
  If Jonson's learned sock be on,
  Or sweetest Shakespeare, fancy's child,
  Warble his native wood-notes wild.'

—' *L'Allegro.*' Which was wrote first?"—*J. Lawson.*

Hopes join'd with doubts, and joys with April tears,
That crowns our love with pleasures : these are gone
When once we come to full fruition.
Like waking in a morning, when all night
Our fancy hath been fed with true delight.
O, what a stroke 'twould be ! sure I should die,
Should I but hear my mistress once say ay.
That monster expectation feeds too high
For any woman e'er to satisfy :
And no brave spirit ever cared for that,
Which in down beds with ease he could come at ;
She's but an honest whore that yields, although
She be as cold as ice, as pure as snow :
He that enjoys her hath no more to say,
But keep us fasting, if you'll have us pray.
Then, fairest mistress, hold the power you have,
By still denying what we still do crave :
In keeping us in hopes strange things to see
That never were, nor are, nor e'er shall be.

A BALLAD.

Upon a Wedding.[1]

I TELL thee, Dick,[2] where I have been,
   Where I the rarest things have seen ;
     O, things without compare !

[1] This ballad was occasioned by the marriage of Roger
Boyle, the first Earl of Orrery (then Lord Broghill), with
Lady Margaret Howard, daughter to Theophilus, Earl of
Suffolk. She was eminently beautiful. Suckling says in
one of his letters, "I know you have but one way (to
teach me to get into love), and will prescribe me now to
look upon Mistress Howard."—*Note in edit.* 1836. [At p.
8 of "Folly in Print, or a Book of Rymes," 1667, attri-
buted to John Raymond, occurs : "Three merry boys of
Kent, to the tune of an old song beginning thus, 'I rode
from England into France,' or to the tune of Sir John
Suckling's Ballad." In "Wit's Recreations," among the
Fancies and Fantasticks (edit. 1817, ii. 405), it is called a
"Ballad," and is accompanied by a woodcut of two plough-

Such sights again cannot be found
In any place on English ground,
    Be it at wake or fair.

At Charing Cross, hard by the way,
Where we (thou know'st) do sell our hay,
    There is a house with stairs ; [1]
And there did I see coming down
Such folk as are not in our town,
    Forty at least, in pairs.

Amongst the rest, one pest'lent fine
(His beard no bigger though than thine)
    Walked on before the rest :
Our landlord looks like nothing to him :
The King (God bless him) 'twould undo him,
    Should he go still so drest.

At Course-a-Park, without all doubt,
He should have first been taken out
    By all the maids i' th' town :

men or rustics, the one narrating, the other listening—
a total misconception of the author's sense. See Hazlitt's
edit. of Lovelace, p. 32. In Patrick Carey's " Trivia," 1651,
edit. 1820, is a poem to the tune of " I tell thee, Dick,
that I have been."]

" This is really excellent, brisk, humorous, witty, and
poetical."—*J. Lawson.* " I fully concur in Mr. Lawson's
criticism, but wish that he had been more explicit. This
[the Ballad] may safely be pronounced his *opus magnum ;*
indeed, for grace and simplicity it stands unrivalled in the
whole compass of ancient or modern poetry."—*W. W.*

[2] [See Lovelace's Poems, 1864, p. 32.]

[1] Suffolk House, originally Northampton, and afterwards
Northumberland, House. The " place where we do sell
our hay" was of course the present Haymarket, and my
uncle, the late Mr. C. W. Reynell, who died January 12,
1892, in his 94th year, told me that he remembered hay
sold there in his early days. Another person, who died
some years since, used to speak to me of a haystack within
his recollection at the bottom of Gray's Inn Lane.

Though lusty Roger there had been,
Or little George upon the Green,
   Or Vincent of the Crown.

But wot you what? the youth was going
To make an end of all his wooing;
   The parson for him stay'd:
Yet by his leave (for all his haste)
He did not so much wish all past
   (Perchance) as did the maid.

The maid (and thereby hangs a tale),[1]
For such a maid no Whitsun-ale
   Could ever yet produce:
No grape, that's kindly ripe, could be
So round, so plump, so soft as she,
   Nor half so full of juice.

Her finger was so small, the ring
Would not stay on, which they did bring,
   It was too wide a peck:
And to say truth (for out it must)
It looked like the great collar (just)
   About our young colt's neck.

Her feet beneath her petticoat,
Like little mice, stole in and out,
   As if they fear'd the light:
But O she dances such a way!
No sun upon an Easter-day
   Is half so fine a sight.

He would have kissed her[2] once or twice,
But she would not, she was so nice,
   She would not do 't in sight,

---

[1] "Moore's description of the beauty of Lilias in the *Loves of the Angels* appears to be an imitation of Suckling."—*Anon.*

[2] "The bashful tenderness of the bride is inimitable. His portraits of female beauty are not so finished as those of Moore and Byron; but they possess greater attraction,

And then she looked as who should say :
I will do what I list to-day,
    And you shall do 't at night.

Her cheeks so rare a white was on,
No daisy makes comparison
    (Who sees them is undone),
For streaks of red were mingled there,
Such as are on a Catherine pear
    (The side that's next the sun).

Her lips were red, and one was thin,
Compar'd to that was next her chin
    (Some bee had stung it newly) ;
But (Dick) her eyes so guard her face ;
I durst no more upon them gaze
    Than on the sun in July.

Her mouth so small, when she does speak,
Thou 'dst swear her teeth her words did break,
    That they might passage get ;
But she so handled still the matter,
They came as good as ours, or better,
    And are not spent a whit.

If wishing should be any sin,
The parson himself had guilty been
    (She look'd that day so purely) ;
And did the youth so oft the feat
At night, as some did in conceit,
    It would have spoiled him surely.

Just in the nick the cook knocked thrice,
And all the waiters in a trice
    His summons did obey ;

because he gives only a glimpse, and leaves the rest to
fancy. Indeed Homer, in describing the peerless Helen,
leaves it almost entirely to the imagination, which is the
great secret of poetry."—*W. W.*

Each serving-man, with dish in hand,
Marched boldly up, like our trained band,
   Presented, and away.

When all the meat was on the table,
What man of knife or teeth was able
   To stay to be entreated?
And this the very reason was,
Before the parson could say grace,
   The company was seated.

The business of the kitchen's great,
For it is fit that men should eat;
   Nor was it there denied:
Passion o' me, how I run on!
There's that that would be thought upon
   (I trow) besides the bride.

Now hats fly off, and youths carouse;[1]
Healths first go round, and then the house,
   The bride's came thick and thick:
And when 'twas nam'd another's health,
Perhaps he made it hers by stealth;
   And who could help it, Dick?

On the sudden up they rise and dance;[2]
Then sit again and sigh, and glance:
   Then dance again and kiss:
Thus several ways the time did pass,
Whilst ev'ry woman wished her place,
   And every man wished his.

By this time all were stol'n aside
To counsel and undress the bride;
   But that he must not know:

[1] "For nature and feeling this passage is above praise."
—*Anon.*
[2] "This stanza is truly beautiful."—*Anon.*

But yet 'twas thought he guess'd her mind,
And did not mean to stay behind
    Above an hour or so.

When in he came (Dick), there she lay
Like new-fall'n snow melting away
    ('Twas time, I trow, to part);
Kisses were now the only stay,
Which soon she gave, as who would say,
    God b' w' ye, with all my heart.

But, just as Heaven would have, to cross it,
In came the bridesmaids with the posset:
    The bridegroom ate in spite;
For had he left the women to 't,
It would have cost two hours to do 't,
    Which were too much that night.

At length the candle 's out, and now
All that they had not done they do.
    What that is, who can tell?
But I believe it was no more
Than thou and I have done before
    With Bridget and with Nell.

M Y dearest rival, lest our love [1]
    Should with eccentric motion move,
Before it learn to go astray,
We'll teach and set it in a way,
And such directions give unto 't,
That it shall never wander foot.
Know first then, we will serve as true
For one poor smile, as we would do,

[1] "This poem, like most of his works, contains great
beauties, alternating with the most childish conceits."-
W. W.

If we had what our higher flame
Or our vainer wish could frame.
Impossible shall be our hope ;
And love shall only have his scope
To join with fancy now and then,
And think what reason would condemn :
And on these grounds we'll love as true,
As if they were most sure t' ensue :
And chastly for these things we'll stay,
As if to-morrow were the day.
Meantime we two will teach our hearts
In love's burdens bear their parts :
Thou first shall sigh, and say she's fair ;
And I'll still answer, past compare.
Thou shalt set out each part o' th' face,
While I extol each little grace ;
Thou shalt be ravish'd at her wit ;
And I, that she so governs it :
Thou shalt like well that hand, that eye,
That lip, that look, that majesty ;
And in good language them adore :
While I want words and do it more.
Yea we will sit and sigh a while,
And with soft thoughts some time beguile,
But straight again break out, and praise
All we had done before, new ways.
Thus will we do till paler death
Come with a warrant for our breath,
And then whose fate shall be to die,
First of us two, by legacy
Shall all his store bequeath, and give
His love to him that shall survive ;
For no one stock can ever serve
To love so much as she'll deserve.

Song.

1.

HONEST lover whatsoever,
    If in all thy love there ever[1]
Was one wav'ring thought, if thy flame
Were not still even, still the same :
      Know this,
      Thou lov'st amiss,
      And to love true,
Thou must begin again, and love anew.

2.

If when she appears i' th' room,
Thou dost not quake, and are struck dumb,
And in striving this to cover,
Dost not speak thy words twice over,
      Know this,
      Thou lov'st amiss,
      And to love true,
Thou must begin again, and love anew.

3.

If fondly thou dost not mistake,
And all defects for graces take,
Persuad'st thyself that jests are broken,
When she hath little or nothing spoken,
      Know this,
      Thou lov'st amiss,
      And to love true,
Thou must begin again, and love anew.

[1] "This poem certainly merits the epithet *sprightly*."—
W. W.

4.

If when thou appearest to be within,
Thou lett'st not men ask and ask again ;
And when thou answerest, if it be,
To what was ask'd thee, properly,
  Know this,
  Thou lov'st amiss,
  And to love true,
Thou must begin again, and love anew.

5.

If when thy stomach calls to eat,
Thou cutt'st not fingers 'stead of meat,
And with much gazing on her face
Dost not rise hungry from the place,
  Know this,
  Thou lov'st amiss,
  And to love true,
Thou must begin again, and love anew.

6.

If by this thou dost discover
That thou art no perfect lover,
And desiring to love true,
Thou dost begin to love anew :
  Know this,
  Thou lov'st amiss,
  And to love true,
Thou must begin again, and love anew.

Upon Two Sisters.

BELIEVE 't young man, I can as eas'ly tell
 How many yards and inches 'tis to hell ;
Unriddle all predestination,

Or the nice points we now dispute upon,
Had the three goddesses been just as fair—
[As . . . and Aglaura are,]¹
It had not been so easily decided,
And sure the apple must have been divided :
It must, it must ; he's impudent, dares say
Which is the handsomer till one's away.
And it was necessary it should be so ;
While Nature did foresee it, and did know,
When she had fram'd the eldest, that each heart
Must at the first sight feel the blind god's dart :
And sure as can be, had she made but one,
No plague had been more sure destruction ;
For we had lik'd, lov'd, burnt to ashes too,
In half the time that we are choosing now :
Variety and equal objects make
The busy eye still doubtful which to take ;
This lip, this hand, this foot, this eye, this face,
The other's body, gesture, or her grace ;
And whilst we thus dispute which of the two,
We unresolv'd go out, and nothing do.
He sure is happiest that has hopes of either,
Next him is he that sees them both together.

To his Rival.

NOW we have taught our love to know,
That it must creep where 't cannot go,
And be for once content to live,
Since here it cannot have to thrive ;
It will not be amiss to inquire
What fuel should maintain this fire :
For fires do either flame too high,
Or where they cannot flame they die.
First then (my half but better heart)

¹ [A line, here supplied by conjecture, is wanting in the editions.]

Know this must wholly be her part;
(For thou and I like clocks are wound
Up to the height, and must move round.)
She then, by still denying what
We fondly crave, shall such a rate
Set on each trifle, that a kiss
Shall come to be the utmost bliss.
Where sparks and fire do meet with tinder,
Those sparks mere fire will still engender:
To make this good, no debt shall be
From service or fidelity;
For she shall ever pay that score,
By only bidding us do more:
So (though she still a niggard be)
In gracing, where none's due, she's free:
The favours she shall cast on us,
(Lest we should grow presumptuous)
Shall not with too much love be shown,
Nor yet the common way still done;
But ev'ry smile and little glance [1]
Shall look half lent, and half by chance:
The ribbon, fan, or muff that she
Would should be kept by thee or me,
Should not be given before too many,
But neither thrown to 's, when there's any;
So that herself should doubtful be
Whether 'twere fortune flung 't, or she.
She shall not like the thing we do
Sometimes, and yet shall like it too;
Nor any notice take at all
Of what, we gone, she would extol:
Love she shall feed, but fear to nourish,
For where fear is, love cannot flourish;
Yet live it must, nay must and shall,
While Desdemona is at all:

[1] "These two lines are very beautiful. The rest of the poem is hardly above mediocrity, but two such lines do not recompense us for a mass of base matter."—*W. W.*

But when she's gone, then love shall die,
And in her grave buried lie.

FAREWELL TO LOVE.[1]

1.

WELL—shadowed landskip, fare ye well:
　　How I have loved you none can tell,
　　At least so well
　As he that now hates more
　Than e'er he loved before.

2.

But, my dear nothings, take your leave,
No longer must you me deceive,
　　Since I perceive
　All the deceit, and know
　Whence the mistake did grow.

3.

As he, whose quicker eye doth trace
A false star shot to a mark'd place,
　　Does run apace,
　And thinking it to catch,
　A jelly up does snatch.

4.

So our dull souls tasting delight
Far off, by sense and appetite
　　Think that is right
　And real good; when yet
　'Tis but the counterfeit.

---

[1] " This ode is inferior to none of his writings for nature
and simplicity, but it partakes of all their faults."—*W. W.*

5.

O, how I glory now, that I
Have made this new discovery !
    Each wanton eye
  Inflamed before : no more
  Will I increase that score.

6.

If I gaze now, 'tis but to see
What manner of death's-head 'twill be,
    When it is free
  From that fresh upper skin,
  The gazer's joy and sin.

7.

The gum and glist'ning which with art
And studied method in each part
    Hangs down the hair,
  Looks (just) as if that day
  Snails there had crawled the hay.

8.

The locks, that curl'd o'er each ear be,
Hang like two master-worms to me,
    That (as we see)
  Have tasted to the rest
  Two holes, where they like 't best.

9.

A quick corse, methink, I spy
In every woman ; and mine eye,
    At passing by,
  Checks, and is troubled, just
  As if it rose from dust.

10.

They mortify, not heighten me :
These of my sins the glasses be :
    And here I see,
How I have loved before,
And so I love no more.

THE INVOCATION.

YE juster powers of Love and Fate,
    Give me the reason why
    A lover cross'd
    And all hopes lost
May not have leave to die.

It is but just, and Love needs must
Confess it is his part,
    When she doth spy
    One wounded lie,
    To pierce the other's heart.

But yet if he so cruel be
To have one breast to hate,
    If I must live
    And thus survive,
    How far more cruel's Fate ?

In this same state I find too late
I am ; and here's the grief :
    Cupid can cure,
    Death heal, I'm sure,
    Yet neither sends relief.

To live or die, beg only I :
Just powers, some end me give ;

And traitor-like
Thus force me not
Without a heart to live.

[A POEM WITH THE ANSWER.]

Sir J. S.

1.

OUT upon it, I have loved
　　Three whole days together;
And am like to love three more,
　　If it prove fair weather.

2.

Time shall moult away his wings,
　　Ere he shall discover
In the whole wide world again
　　Such a constant lover.

3.

But the spite on 't is, no praise
　　Is due at all to me :
Love with me had made no stays,
　　Had it any been but she.

4.

Had it any been but she,
　　And that very face,
There had been at least ere this
　　A dozen dozen in her place.

Sir Toby Matthews.

1.

SAY, but did you love so long?
 In troth, I needs must blame you:
Passion did your judgment wrong,
 Or want of reason shame you.

2.

Truth, time's fair and witty daughter,
 Shortly shall discover,
Y' are a subject fit for laughter,
 And more fool than lover.

3.

But I grant you merit praise
 For your constant folly:
Since you doted three whole days,
 Were you not melancholy?

4.

She to whom you prov'd so true,
 And that very very face,
Puts each minute such as you
 A dozen dozen to disgrace.

Love turned to Hatred.

I WILL not love one minute more, I swear,
 No, not a minute; not a sigh or tear
Thou gett'st from me, or one kind look again,
 Though thou shouldst court me to 't and wouldst
 begin.
I will not think of thee, but as men do
Of debts and sins, and then I'll curse thee too:

For thy sake woman shall be now to me
Less welcome, than at midnight ghosts shall be :
I'll hate so perfectly, that it shall be
Treason to love that man that loves a she ;
Nay, I will hate the very good, I swear,
That's in thy sex, because it doth lie there ;
Their very virtue, grace, discourse and wit,
And all for thee ; what, wilt thou love me yet?

The Careless Lover.

NEVER believe me, if I love,
　　Or know what 'tis, or mean to prove ;
And yet in faith I lie, I do,
And she's extremely handsome too :
　　She's fair, she's wondrous fair,
　　But I care not who know it,
　　Ere I'll die for love, I'll fairly forego it.

This heat of hope, or cold of fear,
My foolish heart could never bear :
One sigh imprisoned ruins more
Than earthquakes have done heretofore :
　　She's fair, &c.

When I am hungry, I do eat,
And cut no fingers 'stead of meat ;
Nor with much gazing on her face
Do e'er rise hungry from the place :
　　She's fair, &c.

A gentle round fill'd to the brink
To this and t' other friend I drink ;
And when 'tis nam'd another's health,
I never make it hers by stealth :
　　She's fair, &c.

Blackfriars to me, and old Whitehall,
Is even as much as is the fall
Of fountains on a pathless grove,
And nourishes as much my love :
    She's fair, &c.

I visit, talk, do business, play,
And for a need laugh out a day :
Who does not thus in Cupid's school,
He makes not love, but plays the fool :
    She's fair, &c.

LOVE AND DEBT ALIKE TROUBLESOME.

THIS one request I make to him that sits the
    clouds above,
That I were freely out of debt, as I am out of love.
Then for to dance, to drink and sing, I should be
    very willing,
I should not owe one lass a kiss, nor ne'er a knave a
    shilling.
'Tis only being in love and debt that breaks us of
    our rest ;
And he that is quite out of both, of all the world is
    blest :
He sees the golden age, wherein all things were free
    and common ;
He eats, he drinks, he takes his rest, he fears no man
    or woman.
Though Crœsus compassed great wealth, yet he still
    craved more,
He was as needy a beggar still, as goes from door to
    door.
Though Ovid were a merry man, love ever kept
    him sad ;
He was as far from happiness as one that is stark
    mad.

Our merchant he in goods is rich, and full of gold
    and treasure ;
But when he thinks upon his debts, that thought
    destroys his pleasure.
Our courtier thinks that he's preferred, whom every
    man envies ;
When love so rumbles in his pate, no sleep comes in
    his eyes.
Our gallant's case is worst of all, he lies so just be-
    twixt them ;
For he's in love and he's in debt, and knows not
    which most vex'th him.
But he that can eat beef, and feed on bread which
    is so brown,
May satisfy his appetite, and owe no man a crown :
And he that is content with lasses clothed in plain
    woollen,
May cool his heat in every place, he need not to be
    sullen,
Nor sigh for love of lady fair ; for this each wise
    man knows
As good stuff under flannel lies, as under silken
    clothes.

Song.

I PRITHEE send me back my heart,
    Since I cannot have thine :
For if from yours you will not part,
    Why then shouldst thou have mine ?

Yet now I think on't, let it lie,
    To find it were in vain,
For th' hast a thief in either eye
    Would steal it back again.

Why should two hearts in one breast lie,
    And yet not lodge together ?

O love, where is thy sympathy,
   If thus our breasts thou sever?

But love is such a mystery,
   I cannot find it out:
For when I think I'm best resolv'd,
   I then am in most doubt.

Then farewell care, and farewell woe,
   I will no longer pine:
For I'll believe I have her heart,
   As much as she hath mine.

To a Lady that forbade to Love before Company.[1]

WHAT! no more favours? Not a ribbon more,
   Not fan nor muff to hold as heretofore?
Must all the little blisses then be left,
And what was once love's gift, become our theft?
May we not look ourselves into a trance,
Teach our souls parley at our eyes, not glance,
Not touch the hand, not by soft wringing there
Whisper a love that only yes can hear?
Not free a sigh, a sigh that's there for you?
Dear, must I love you, and not love you too?
Be wise, nice, fair; for sooner shall they trace
The feather'd choristers from place to place,
By prints they make in th' air, and sooner say
By what right line the last star made his way,
That fled from heaven to earth, than guess to know
How our loves first did spring, or how they grow.
Love is all spirit: fairies sooner may
Be taken tardy, when they night-tricks play,
Than we, we are too dull and lumpish rather,
Would they could find us both in bed together!

[1] Cibber, in his "Lives of the Poets," considers these as Suckling's best lines. I cannot coincide with him in this criticism.—*Note in edition* 1836.

The Guiltless Inconstant.

MY first love, whom all beauties did adorn,
    Firing my heart, suppress'd it with her scorn;
Since like the tinder in my breast it lies,
By every sparkle made a sacrifice.
Each wanton eye can kindle my desire,
And that is free to all which was entire;
Desiring more by the desire I lost,
As those that in consumptions linger most.
And now my wand'ring thoughts are not confin'd
Unto one woman, but to womankind:
This for her shape I love, that for her face,
This for her gesture, or some other grace:
And where that none of all these things I find,
I choose her by the kernel, not the rind:
And so I hope since my first hope is gone,
To find in many what I lost in one;
And like to merchants after some great loss,
Trade by retail, that cannot do in gross.
The fault is hers that made me go astray,
He needs must wander that hath lost his way:
Guiltless I am; she doth this change provoke,
And made that charcoal, which to her was oak,
And as a looking-glass from the aspect
Whilst it is whole, doth but one face reflect;
But being crack'd or broken, there are grown
Many less faces, where there was but one:
So love unto my heart did first prefer
Her image, and there placed none but her;
But since 'twas broke and marty'd by her scorn,
Many less faces in her place are born.

Love's Representation.

LEANING her head upon my breast,
    There on love's bed she lay to rest;

My panting heart rock'd her asleep,
My heedful eyes the watch did keep ;
Then love by me being harbour'd there,
In[1] hope to be his harbinger,
Desire his rival kept the door ;
For this of him I begg'd no more,
But that, our mistress to entertain,
Some pretty fancy he would frame,
And represent it in a dream,
Of which myself should give the theme.
Then first these thoughts I bid him show,
Which only he and I did know,
Arrayed in duty and respect,
And not in fancies that reflect,
Then those of value next present,
Approv'd by all the world's consent ;
But to distinguish mine asunder,
Apparell'd they must be in wonder.
Such a device then I would have,
As service, not reward, should crave,
Attir'd in spotless innocence,
Not self-respect, nor no pretence :
Then such a faith I would have shown,
As heretofore was never known.
Cloth'd with a constant clear intent,
Professing always as it meant.
And if love no such garments have,
My mind a wardrobe is so brave,
That there sufficient he may see
To clothe Impossibility.
Then beamy fetters he shall find,
By admiration subtly twin'd,
That will keep fast the wanton'st thought,
That o'er imagination wrought :
There he shall find of joy a chain,
Framed by despair of her disdain,

[1] [Old copy, *No.*]

So curiously that it can't tie
The smallest hopes that thoughts now spy.
There acts, as glorious as the sun,
Are by her veneration spun,
In one of which I would have brought
A pure, unspotted abstract thought.
Considering her as she is good,
Not in her frame of flesh and blood.
These atoms then, all in her sight,
I bade him join, that so he might
Discern between true love's creation,
And that love's form that's now in fashion.
Love granting unto my request
Began to labour in my breast;
But with this motion he did make,
It heav'd so high that she did wake.
Blush'd at the favour she had done,
Then smil'd, and then away did run.

SONG.

THE crafty boy that had full oft assay'd
  To pierce my stubborn and resisting breast,
But still the bluntness of his darts betrayed,
Resolv'd at last of setting up his rest,
    Either my wild unruly heart to tame,
    Or quit his godhead, and his bow disclaim.

So all his lovely looks, his pleasing fires;
All his sweet motions, all his taking smiles;
All that awakes, all that inflames desires,
All that by sweet commands, all that beguiles,
    He does into one pair of eyes convey,
    And there begs leave that he himself may stay.

And there he brings me, where his ambush lay,
Secure and careless, to a stranger land;

And never warning me, which was foul play,
Does make me close by all this beauty stand.
    Where first struck dead, I did at last recover,
    To know that I might only live to love her.

So I'll be sworn I do, and do confess,
The blind lad's power, whilst he inhabits there;
But I'll be even with him nevertheless,
If e'er I chance to meet with him elsewhere.
    If other eyes invite the boy to tarry,
    I'll fly to hers as to a sanctuary.

Upon the Black Spots worn by my Lady D. E.[1]

Madam,

I KNOW your heart cannot so guilty be,
    That you should wear those spots for vanity;
Or as your beauty's trophies, put on one
For every murder which your eyes have done:
No, they're your mourning-weeds for hearts forlorn
Which, though you must not love, you could not
    scorn;
To whom since cruel honour doth deny
Those joys could only cure their misery;
Yet you this noble way to grace them found,
Whilst thus our grief their martyrdom hath crown'd.
Of which take heed you prove not prodigal,
For if to every common funeral,
By your eyes martyr'd, such grace were allow'd,
Your face would wear not patches, but a cloud.

Song.

IF you refuse me once and think again,
    I will complain.

[1] [Could this be the Dorothy Enion who married Stanley the poet? See Hammond's Poems, 1655, edition 1816, p. 34, and Lovelace's Poems, edition 1864, pp. 227-8.]

You are deceiv'd, love is no work of art,
    It must be got and born,
    Not made and worn,
By every one that hath a heart.

Or do you think they more than once can die,
    Whom you deny.
Who tell you of a thousand deaths a day,
    Like the old poets feign
    And tell the pain
They met, but in the common way.

Or do you think 't too soon to yield,
    And quit the field.
Nor is that right, they yield that first entreat ;
    Once one may crave for love,
    But more would prove
This heart too little, that too great.

O that I were all soul, that I might prove
    For you as fit a love,
As you are for an angel ; for I know,
None but pure spirits are fit loves for you.

You are all ethereal, there is no dross,
    Nor any part that's gross.
Your coarsest part is like a curious lawn,
The vestal relics for a covering dawn.

Your other parts, part of the purest fire
    That e'er Heaven did inspire ;
Makes every thought that is refined by it,
A quintessence of goodness and of wit.

Thus have your raptures reach'd to that degree
    In Love's philosophy,
That you can figure to yourself a fire
Void of all heat, a love without desire.

Nor in Divinity do you go less :
        You think, and you profess,
That souls may have a plenitude of joy,
Although their bodies meet not to employ.

But I must needs confess, I do not find
        The motions of my mind
So purified as yet, but at the best
My body claims in them an interest.

I hold that perfect joy makes all our parts
        As joyful as our hearts.
Our senses tell us if we please not them,
Our love is but a dotage or a dream.

How shall we then agree? you may descend,
        But will not, to my end.
I fain would tune my fancy to your key,
But cannot reach to that obstructed way.

There rests but this, that whilst we sorrow here,
        Our bodies may draw near :
And when no more their joys they can extend,
Then let our souls begin where they did end.

PROFFERED LOVE REJECTED.

IT is not four years ago,
    I offered forty crowns
To lie with her a night or so :
    She answer'd me in frowns.

Not two years since, she meeting me
    Did whisper in my ear,
That she would at my service be,
    If I contented were.

I told her I was cold as snow,
   And had no great desire ;
But should be well content to go
   To twenty, but no higher.

Some three months since or thereabout,
   She that so coy had been,
Bethought herself and found me out,
   And was content to sin.

I smil'd at that, and told her I
   Did think it something late,
And that I'd not repentance buy
   At above half the rate.

This present morning early she
   Forsooth came to my bed,
And *gratis* there she offered me
   Her high-priz'd maidenhead.

I told her that I thought it then
   Far dearer than I did,
When I at first the forty crowns
   For one night's lodging bid.

DESDAIN.

1.

A QUOY servent tant d'artifices
   Et servens aux vents iettez,
Si vos amours et vos services
   Me sont des importunitez.

2.

L'amour a d'autres vœux m'appelle ;
   N'tendez jamais rien de moy,

Ne pensez nous rendre infidele,
  A mi tesmoignant vostre foy.

3.

L'amant qui mon amour possede
  Est trop plein de perfection,
Et doublement il vous excede
  De merit et d'affection.

4.

Je ne puis estre refroidie,
  Ni rompre un cordage si doux,
Ni le rompre sans perfidie,
  Ni d'estre perfide pour vous.

5.

Vos attentes sont toutes en vain,
  Le vous dire est vous obliger,
Pour vous faire espargner vos peines
  Des vœux et du temps mesnager.

Englished thus by the Author.

1.

TO what end serve the promises
  And oaths lost in the air,
Since all your proffer'd services
  To me but tortures are?

2.

Another now enjoys my love,
  Set you your heart at rest:
Think not me from my faith to move,
  Because you faith protest.

3.

The man that does possess my heart,
　Has twice as much perfection,
And does excel you in desert,
　As much as in affection.

4.

I cannot break so sweet a bond,
　Unless I prove untrue :
Nor can I ever be so fond,
　To prove untrue for you.

· 5.

Your attempts are but in vain
　(To tell you is a favour) :
For things that may be, rack your brain :
　Then lose not thus your labour.

LUTEA ALLISON :

Si sola es, nulla es.

THOUGH you Diana-like have liv'd still chaste,
　Yet must you not (fair) die a maid at last :
The roses on your cheeks were never made
To bless the eye alone, and so to fade ;
Nor had the cherries on your lips their being
To please no other sense than that of seeing :
You were not made to look on, though that be
A bliss too great for poor mortality :
In that alone those rarer parts you have,
To better uses sure wise nature gave
Than that you put them to ; to love, to wed :
For Hymen's rights and for the marriage-bed
You were ordained, and not to lie alone ;
One is no number, till that two be one.

To keep a maidenhead till but fifteen,
Is worse than murder, and a greater sin
Than to have lost it in the lawful sheets
With one that should want skill to reap those
    sweets :
But not to lose 't at all—by Venus, this,
And by her son, inexpiable is ;
And should each female guilty be o' th' crime,
The world would have its end before its time.

PERJURY EXCUSED.

ALAS, it is too late ! I can no more
    Love now than I have loved before :
My Flora, 'tis my fate, not I :
And what you call contempt, is destiny.
I am no monster, sure, I cannot show
Two hearts ; one I already owe ;
And I have bound myself with oaths, and vowed
Oftener I fear than Heaven hath e'er allowed,
That faces now should work no more on me,
Than if they could not charm, or I not see.
And shall I break them ? shall I think you can
Love, if I could, so foul a perjur'd man ?
O no, 'tis equally impossible that I
Should love again, or you love perjury.

A SONG.[1]

HAST thou seen the down in the air
    When wanton blasts have tossed it ?
Or the ship on the sea,
    When ruder winds have crossed it ?
Hast thou marked the crocodile's weeping,
    Or the fox's sleeping ?

[1] "This is an imitation of a song in Ben Jonson's
'Devil is an Ass,' Act ii. sc. 2."—*Anon.*

Or hast viewed the peacock in his pride,
　　　Or the dove by his bride,
　　　When he courts for his lechery ?
O, so fickle, O, so vain, O, so false, so false is she?

Upon T[homas] C[arew] having the Pox.

TROTH, Tom, I must confess I much admire
　　　Thy water should find passage through the
　　　　fire ;
For fire and water never could agree,
These now by nature have some sympathy :
Sure then his way he forces, for all know
The French ne'er grants a passage to his foe.
If it be so, his valour I must praise,
That being weaker, yet can force his ways ;
And wish that to his valour he had strength,
That he might drive the fire quite out at length ;
For, troth, as yet the fire gets the day,
For evermore the water runs away.

Upon the First Sight oy my Lady Seymour.

WONDER not much, if thus amazed I look,
　　　Since I saw you, I have been planet-struck:
A beauty and so rare I did descry,
As, should I set her forth, you all, as I,
Would lose your hearts ; for he that can
Know her and live, he must be more than man.
An apparition of so sweet a creature,
That, credit me, she had not any feature
That did not speak her angel. But no more
Such heavenly things as these we must adore,
Nor prattle of ; lest, when we do but touch,
Or strive to know, we wrong her too-too much.

Upon L[ady] M[iddlesex] Weeping.

WHOEVER was the cause your tears were shed,
   May these my curses light upon his head :
May he be first in love, and let it be
With a most known and black deformity,
Nay, far surpass all witches that have been,
Since our first parents taught us how to sin !
Then let this hag be coy, and he run mad
For that which no man else would e'er have had ;
And in this fit may he commit the thing
May him impenitent to the gallows bring !
Then might he for one tear his pardon have,
But want that single grief his life to save !
And being dead, may he at heaven venter,
But for the guilt of this one fact ne'er enter.

The Deformed Mistress.

I KNOW there are some fools that care
   Not for the body, so the face be fair ;
Some others, too, that in a female creature
Respect not beauty, but a comely feature ;
And others, too, that for those parts in sight
Care not so much, so that the rest be right.
Each man his humour hath, and faith 'tis mine
To love a woman which I now define.
First I would have her wainscot-foot and hand
More wrinkled far than any plaited band,
That in those furrows, if I'd take the pains,
I might both sow and reap all sorts of grains :
Her nose I'd have a foot long, not above,
With pimples embroidered, for those I love ;
And at the end a comely pearl of snot,
Considering whether it should fall or not :
Provided, next, that half her teeth be out,
Nor do I care much if her pretty snout

E

Meet with her furrowed chin, and both together
Hem in her lips, as dry as good white leather.
One wall-eye she shall have ; for that's a sign
In other beasts the best, why not in mine ?
Her neck I'll have to be pure jet at least,
With yellow spots enamelled ; and her breast,
Like a grasshopper's wing, both thin and lean,
Not to be touched for dirt, unless swept clean.
As for her belly, 'tis no matter so
There be a belly, and a c—— also.
Yet if you will, let it be something high,
And always let there be a timpany—
But soft ! where am I now ? here I should stride,
Lest I fall in, the place must be so wide,
And pass unto her thighs, which shall be just
Like to an ant's that's scraping in the dust.
Into her legs I'd have love's issue fall,
And all her calf into a gouty small :
Her feet both thick and eagle-like displayed,
The symptoms of a comely, handsome maid.
As for her parts behind, I ask no more,
If they but answer those that are before,
I have my utmost wish : and having so,
Judge whether I am happy—yea or no.

Upon Mrs. A. L.[1]

Non est mortale quod opto.

THOU think'st I flatter, when thy praise I tell,
    But thou dost all hyperboles excel ;
For I am sure thou art no mortal creature,
But a divine one, throned in human feature.
Thy piety is such, that heaven by merit,
If ever any did, thou shouldst inherit.
Thy modesty is such, that hadst thou been
Tempted as Eve, thou wouldst have shunned her sin.

[1 See Lovelace's Poems, edit. 1864, pp. 126, 127.]

So lovely fair thou art, that sure Dame Nature
Meant thee the pattern of the female creature.
Besides all this, thy flowing wit is such,
That were it not in thee, it had been too much
For womankind : should envy look thee o'er,
It would confess thus much, if not much more.
I love thee well, yet wish some bad in thee,
For sure I am thou art too good for me.

HIS DREAM.

ON a still, silent night, scarce could I number
    One of the clock, but that a golden slumber
Had locked my senses fast, and carried me
Into a world of blest felicity,
I know not how : first to a garden, where
The apricot, the cherry, and the pear,
The strawberry and plum, were fairer far
Than that eye-pleasing fruit that caused the jar
Betwixt the goddesses, and tempted more
Than fair Atlanta's ball, though gilded o'er.
I gazed awhile on these, and presently
A silver stream ran softly gliding by,
Upon whose banks, lilies more white than snow,
New fallen from heaven, with violets mixed, did
    grow ;
Whose scent so chafed the neighbour-air, that you
Would softly swear that Arabic spices grew
Not far from thence, or that the place had been
With musk prepared, to entertain Love's queen.
Whilst I admired, the river passed away,
And up a grove did spring, green as in May
When April had been moist ; upon whose bushes
·The pretty robins, nightingales, and thrushes
Warbled their notes so sweetly, that my ears
Did judge at least the music of the spheres.
But here my gentle dream conveyed me
Into the place where I most longed to see,

My mistress' bed ; who, some few blushes past
And smiling frowns, contented was at last
To let me touch her neck ; I, not content
With that, slipped to her breast, thence lower went,
And then I—— awaked.

Upon A. M.

YIELD all my love ; but be withal as coy,
    As if thou knew'st not how to sport and toy :
The fort resigned with ease, men cowards prove
And lazy grow.   Let me besiege my love,
Let me despair at least three times a day,
And take repulses upon each essay ;
If I but ask a kiss, straight blush as red
As if I tempted for thy maidenhead :
Contract thy smiles, if that they go too far,
And let thy frowns be such as threaten war.
That face which nature sure never intended
Should e'er be marred, because 't could ne'er be
    mended.
Take no corruption from thy grandame Eve ;
Rather want faith to save thee, than believe
Too soon ; for credit me 'tis true,
Men most of all enjoy, when least they do.

A Candle.

THERE is a thing which in the light
    Is seldom used, but in the night
It serves the maiden female crew,
The ladies, and the good-wives too.
They use to take it in their hand,
And then it will uprightly stand ;
And to a hole they it apply,
Where by its goodwill it would die ;
It spends, goes out, and still within
It leaves its moisture thick and thin.

The Metamorphosis.

THE little boy, to show his might and power,
  Turn'd Io to a cow, Narcissus to a flower;
Transformed Apollo to a homely swain,
And Jove himself into a golden rain.
These shapes were tolerable, but by the mass
He's metamorphosed me into an ass.

To B. C.

WHEN first, fair mistress, I did see your face,
  I brought, but carried no eyes from the
    place:
And since that time god Cupid hath me led,
In hope that once I shall enjoy your bed.
  But I despair; for now, alas! I find,
  Too late for me, the blind does lead the blind.

Upon Sir John Laurence's bringing Water over the Hills to my L. Middlesex's House at Witten.

AND is the water come? sure 't cannot be,
  It runs too much against philosophy;
For heavy bodies to the centre bend,
Light bodies only naturally ascend.
How comes this then to pass? The good knight's
  skill
Could nothing do without the water's will:
  Then 'twas the water's love that made it flow,
  For love will creep where well it cannot go.

A Barber.

I AM a barber and, I'd have you know,
  A shaver too, sometimes no mad one though;

The reason why you see me now thus bare,
Is 'cause I always trade against the hair.
But yet I keep a state ; who comes to me,
Whosoe'er he is, he must uncover'd be.
When I'm at work, I'm bound to find discourse,
To no great purpose, of great Sweden's force,
Of Witel, and the Bourse, and what 'twill cost
To get that back which was this summer lost.
So fall to praising of his Lordship's hair :
Ne'er so deform'd, I swear 'tis *sans* compare.
I tell him that the King's doth sit no fuller,
And yet his is not half so good a colour ;
Then reach a pleasing glass, that's made to lie,
Like to its master, most notoriously ;
And if he must his mistress see that day,
I with a powder send him straight away.

A Soldier.

I AM a man of war and might,
  And know thus much, that I can fight,
Whether I am i' th' wrong or right,
              Devoutly.

No woman under heaven I fear,
New oaths I can exactly swear,
And forty healths my brain will bear
              Most stoutly.

I cannot speak, but I can do
As much as any of our crew ;
And if you doubt it, some of you
              May prove me.

I dare be bold thus much to say,
If that my bullets do but play,
You would be hurt so night and day,
              Yet love me.

To my Lady E. C. at her going out of England.

I MUST confess, when I did part from you,
  I could not force an artificial dew
Upon my cheeks, nor with a gilded phrase
Express how many hundred several ways
My heart was tortur'd, nor with arms across
In discontented garbs set forth my loss :
Such loud expressions many times do come
From lightest hearts : great griefs are always dumb.
The shallow rivers roar, the deep are still.
Numbers of painted words may show much skill,
But little anguish and a cloudy face
Is oft put on, to serve both time and place
The blazing wood may to the eye seem great,
But 'tis the fire rak'd up that has the heat,
And keeps it long.   True sorrow's like to wine,
That which is good, does never need a sign.
My eyes were channels far too small to be
Conveyers of such floods of misery.
And so pray think, or if you'd entertain
A thought more charitable, suppose some strain
Of sad repentance had, not long before,
Quite emptied for my sins that watery store.
So shall you him oblige that still will be
You servant to his best ability.

A Pedlar of Smallwares.

A PEDLAR I am, that take great care
  And mickle pains for to sell smallware :
I had need do so, when women do buy,
That in smallwares trade so unwillingly.

L. W.

A looking-glass, wilt please you, madam, buy ?
A rare one 'tis indeed, for in it I

Can show what all the world besides can't do,
A face like to your own, so fair, so true.

L. E.

For you a girdle, madam ; but I doubt me
Nature hath order'd there's no waist about ye ;
Pray, therefore, be but pleas'd to search my pack,
There's no ware that I have that you shall lack.

L. E.   L. M.

You ladies, want you pins? if that you do,
I have those will enter, and that stiffly too :
It's time you choose, in troth ; you will bemoan
Too late your tarrying, when my pack's once gone.

L. B.   L. A.

As for you, ladies, there are those behind
Whose ware perchance may better take your mind :
One cannot please ye all ; the pedlar will draw back,
And wish against himself, that you may have the
    knack.

An Answer to some Verses made in his Praise.

THE ancient poets and their learned rhymes
    We still admire in these our later times,
And celebrate their fames.   Thus, though they die,
Their names can never taste mortality :
Blind Homer's muse and Virgil's stately verse,
While any live, shall never need a hearse.
Since then to these such praise was justly due
For what they did, what shall be said to you?
These had their helps ; they wrote of gods and
    kings,
Of temples, battles, and of such gallant things :
But you of nothing ; how could you have writ,
Had you but chose a subject to your wit?

To praise Achilles or the Trojan crew,
Showed little art, for praise was but their due.
To say she's fair that's fair, this is no pains:
He shows himself most poet, that most feigns:
To find out virtues strangely hid in me;
Ay, there's the art and learned poetry!
To make one striding of a barbed steed,
Prancing a stately round: I use indeed
To ride Bat Jewel's jade; this is the skill,
This shows the poet wants not wit at will.
    I must admire aloof, and for my part
    Be well contented, since you do 't with art.

LOVE'S BURNING-GLASS.

WONDERING long, how could I harmless see
    Men gazing on those beams that fired me;
At last I found it was the crystal-love
Before my heart, that did the heat improve:
Which, by contracting of those scatter'd rays
Into itself, did so produce my blaze.
Now lighted by my love, I see the same
Beams dazzle those, that me are wont t' inflame.
And now I bless my love, when I do think
By how much I had rather burn than wink.
But how much happier were it thus to burn,
If I had liberty to choose my urn!
But since those beams do promise only fire,
This flame shall purge me of the dross—desire.

THE MIRACLE.

IF thou be'st ice, I admire
    How thou couldst set my heart on fire;
Or how thy fire could kindle me,
Thou being ice, and not melt thee;
But even my flames, light as thy own,
Have hardened thee into a stone!

Wonder of love that canst fulfil,
Inverting nature thus, thy will ;
Making ice one another burn,
Whilst itself doth harder turn.

Εἰ μὲν ἦν μαθεῖν
Ἁ δεῖ παθεῖν
Καὶ μὴ παθεῖν
Καλὸν ἦν τὸ μαθεῖν
Εἰ δὲ δεῖ παθεῖν
Ἁ δεῖ μαθεῖν
Τί δεῖ μαθεῖν
Χρῆ γὰρ παθεῖν.

Scire si liceret quæ debes subire,
Et non subire, pulcrum est scire :
Sed si subire debes quæ debes scire :
Quersum vis scire, nam debes subire ?

Englished thus—

If man might know
     The ill he must undergo,
And shun it so,
     Then it were good to know :
But if he undergo it,
     Though he know it,
What boots him know it ?
     He must undergo it.

SONG.

WHEN, dearest, I but think of thee,
     Methinks all things that lovely be
Are present, and my soul delighted :
For beauties that from worth arise
Are like the grace of deities,
Still present with us, though unsighted.

Thus whilst I sit, and sigh the day
With all his borrowed lights away,
Till night's black wings do overtake me,
Thinking on thee, thy beauties then,
As sudden lights do sleeping men,
So they by their bright rays awake me.

Thus absence dies, and dying proves
No absence can subsist with loves
That do partake of fair perfection ;
Since in the darkest night they may
By love's quick motion find a way
To see each other by reflection.

The waving sea can with each flood
Bathe some high promont that hath stood
Far from the main up in the river :
O, think not then but love can do
As much, for that's an ocean too,
Which flows not every day, but ever !

The Expostulation.

TELL me, ye juster deities,
    That pity lovers' miseries,
Why should my own unworthiness
Fright me to seek my happiness ?
It is as natural as just
Him for to love, whom needs I must :
All men confess that love's a fire,
Then who denies it to aspire ?

Tell me, if thou wert fortune's thrall,
Would'st thou not raise thee from the fall ?
Seek only to o'erlook thy state.
Whereto thou art condemned by fate ?
Then let me love my Coridon,
And by love's leave, leave him alone :

For I have read of stories oft,
That love hath wings. and soars aloft.

Then let me grow in my desire,
Though I be martyr'd in that fire ;
For grace it is enough for me,
But only to love such as he :
For never shall my thoughts be base,
Though luckless, yet without disgrace :
Then let him that my love shall blame,
Or clip love's wings, or quench love's flame.

DETRACTION EXECRATED.

THOU vermin slander, bred in abject minds
    Of thoughts impure, by vile tongues animate,
Canker of conversation ! couldst thou find
Nought but our love whereon to show thy hate ?
Thou never wert when we two were alone ;
What canst thou witness then ? thy base dull aid
Was useless in our conversation,
Where each meant more than could by both be said.
Whence hadst thou thy intelligence ; from earth ?
That part of us ne'er knew that we did love :
Or from the air ?   Our gentle sighs had birth
From such sweet raptures as to joy did move :
Our thoughts,   as   pure   as   the   chaste   morning's
     breath,
When from the night's cold arms it creeps away,
Were cloth'd in words; and maiden's blush that
     hath
More purity, more innocence than they.
Nor from the water couldst thou have this tale,
No briny tear hath furrow'd her smooth cheek,
And I was pleased ; I pray what snould he ail
That had her love, for what else could he seek ?
We shortened days to moments by love's art,

Whilst our two souls in amorous ecstasy
Perceived no passing time, as if a part
Our love had been of still eternity.
Much less could have it from the purer fire :
Our heat exhales no vapour from the coarse sense,
Such as are hopes, or fears, or fond desires ;
Our mutual love itself did recompense.
Thou hast no correspondence in heaven
And th' elemental world thou seest is free :
Whence hadst thou then this talking, monster ?
    even
From hell, a harbour fit for it and thee.
Curst be th' officious tongue that did address
Thee to her ears, to ruin my content :
May it one minute taste such happiness,
Deserving lose 't, unpitied it lament !
I must forbear her sight, and so repay
In grief those hours joy shortened to a dram :
Each minute I will lengthen to a day,
And in one year outlive Methusalem.

SONG.

UNJUST decrees, that do at once exact
    From such a love as worthy hearts should own
        So wild a passion,
      And yet so tame a presence
        As holding no proportion,
  Changes into impossible obedience.

Let it suffice, that neither I do love
In such a calm observance as to weigh
        Each word I say,
    And each examined look t' approve
      That towards her doth move,
        Without so much of fire
As might in time kindle into desire.

Or give me leave to burst into a flame,
And at the scope of my unbounded will
      Love her my fill,
    No superscriptions of fame,
    Of honour, or good name,
      No thought but to improve
The gentle and quick approaches of my love.

But thus to throng, and overlade a soul
With love, and then to leave a room for fear,
     That shall all that control,
     What is it but to rear
   Our passions and our hopes on high,
     That thence they may descry
The noblest way how to despair and die ?

A Prologue of the Author's to a Masque at Witten.

EXPECT not here a curious river fine,
   Our wits are short of that : alas the time !
The neat refined language of the court
We know not ; if we did, our country sport
Must not be too ambitious ; 'tis for kings,
Not for their subjects, to have such rare things.
Besides though, I confess, Parnassus hardly,
Yet Helicon this summer-time is dry :
Our wits were at an ebb or very low,
And, to say troth, I think they cannot flow.
But yet a gracious influence from you
May alter nature in our brow-sick crew.
Have patience, then, we pray, and sit a while,
And, if a laugh be too much, lend a smile.

CANTILENA POLITICA-JOCUNDA FACTA POST PRIN-
CIPIS DISCESSUM IN HISPANIAM, 1623.[1]

I COME from England into France
Neither to learn to sing nor dance,
Nor yet to ride nor fence;
Nor yet to see strange things as those,
Which have returned without the nose,
They carried out from hence.
But I to Paris rode along
Just[2] like John Dory in the song,
Upon an holy tide;
For I an ambling nag did get,
I hope he is not paid for yet,
I spurred him on each side.
And to St. Denis first I came
To see the sights at Notre Dame,
The man that showeth snuffles;
Where who is apt for to believe,
May see St. Mary's right-hand sleeve,
And her old pantuffles:
Her breast, her milk, her very gown,
Which she did wear in Bethlehem town,
When in the inn she lay.
That all the world knows is a fable,
For so good clothes ne'er lay in stable
Upon a lock of hay.
Nor carpenter could by his trade
Gain so much coin as to have made
A gown[3] of such rich stuff:

[1] [Not in the editions. Now printed from Harl. MS.,
367, where it is anonymous, but in the handwriting of the
late Sir Henry Ellis is attributed to Suckling. There is
little doubt that it is his. If so, it was a very early production, even if (which is probable) it was not written
quite so early as 1623. On the back is the endorsement:
Cantilena de Gallico itinere, 1623.] [2 MS., *nist.*]

[3 Orig. *gayne*—which, after all, may be right, allowing
for local pronunciation.]

Yet they (poor souls) think for her credit,
They must believe old Joseph did it,
      'Cause he deserved enough.
There is one of the Cross's nails,
Which whoso sees his bonnet vails,
      And (if he will) may kneel.
Some say 'twas false, 'twas never so;
But, feeling it, this much I know,
      It is as true as steel!
There is the lanthorn, which the Jews,
When Judas led them forth, did use;
      It weighs my weight down-right:
Yet, to believe it, you must think
The Jews did put a candle in 't:
      And then 'twas wondrous light.
There's one saint there did lose his nose,
Another 's head, another 's toes,
      An elbow and a thumb.
But when we had seen these holy rags,
We went to our inn, and took our nags,
      And so away did come.
I came to Paris on the Seine;
'Twas wonderous fair, but little clean;
      'Tis Europe's greatest town.
How strange it is, I need not tell it,
For all the world may easily smell it,
      As they pass up and down.
There's many strange things for to see:
The Palace, the great Gallery;
      Place Royal doth excel;
The new bridge and the statue there,
At Notre Dame, St. Christopher,
      The steeple bears the bell.
For learning the University,
And for old clothes the Frippery—
      That house the queen did build.
St. Innocent, whose teeth devours
Dead corpse in four-and-twenty hours,
      And there the king was kill'd.

The Bastern and St. Denis Street;
The Spital, like to London Fleet;
  The Arsenal, no toy.
But if you'll see the prettiest thing,
You must go to court, and see the king :[1]
  O, 'tis a hopeful boy!
For he by all his dukes and peers
Is reverenced for wit as mnch as years,
  Nor may you think it much;
For he with little switch can play,
And can make fine dirt-pies of clay :
  O, never king made such!
A bird, that can but kill a fly,
Or prates, doth please his Majesty,
  'Tis known to every one.
The Duke of Guise gave him a parrot,
And he had twenty cannons for it,
  And a great galleon.
O, that I e'er might have the hap
To get the bird within the map
  'Tis called the Indian Roc!
I'd give it him, and look to be
  As great and wise as Luisuè,[2]
  Or else I had hard luck.
Birds [a]round his chamber stands,
And he them feeds with his own hands—
  'Tis his humility :
And if that they want anything,
They may go whistle for their king,
  And he'll come presently.
Besides all this he hath a jerk,
Taught him by nature for to work
  In iron with great ease.

[1] Lewis XIII., son to Henry IV., styled Great Henry.—
Note in MS.
[2] Marques de Luines was his favourite, who died miserably during the last year's siege of Mountabö, 1622.—*Note in MS.*

Sometimes into his forge he goes,
And there he puffs and there he blows,
　　　　　And makes both locks and keys ;
Which puts a doubt in every one,
Whether he were Mars' or Vulcan's son—
　　　　　Some few believes his mother ;
But yet let all say what they will,
I am resolved, and will think still,
　　　　　As much the one as the other.
The people do mislike the youth,
Alleging reasons for a truth,
　　　　　Mothers should honoured be ;
Yet some believe he loves her rather,
As well as she did love his father,
　　　　　And that notoriously.
'Tis charity for to be known,
Loves others' children as his own ;
　　　　　Nor must you think it shame ;
Unless that he would greater be
Than was his father Henry,
　　　　　Whose thoughts ne'er did the same.

VERSES.[1]

I AM confirm'd a woman can
　　Love this, or that, or any other man ;
This days she's melting hot,
To-morrow swears she knows you not ;
If she but a new object find,
Then straight she's of another mind.
　　Then hang me, ladies, at your door,
　　If e'er I dote upon you more.

Yet still I love the fairsome (why ?
For nothing but to please my eye) ;

[1] [Communicated to *Notes and Queries*, 1st series, i. 72, by A[lexander] D[yce ?]. The writer states that he found them in a small 4to volume of English poetry, *temp.* Charles I. They are there called "Sir John Suckling's Verses."]

And so the fat and soft-skinn'd dame
I'll flatter to appease my flame ;
For she that's musical I'll long,
When I am sad to sing a song,
   Then hang me, ladies, at your door
   If e'er I dote upon you more.

I'll give my fancy leave to range
Through everywhere to find out change ;
The black, the brown, the fair shall be
But objects of variety ;
I'll court you all to serve my turn,
But with such flames as shall not burn.
   Then hang me, ladies, at your door,
   If e'er I dote upon you more.

SIR JOHN SUCKLING'S ANSWER.[1]

I TELL thee, fellow, whoe'er thou be,
   That made this fine sing-song of me,
      Thou art a rhyming sot ;
These very lines do thee bewray,
This barren wit makes all men say,
      'Twas some rebellious Scot.

But its no wonder that you sing
Such songs of me, who am no king,
      When every Blue Cap swears
He'll not obey King James his ba'rn,
That hugs a bishop under his arm,
      And hangs them in his ears.

Had I been of your covenant,
You would have call'd me John of Gaunt,
      And given me great renown.

---

[1] [Ashm. MS., 36, fol. 54. Now first printed? See what has been said in the Introduction.]

But now I am John for the King,
You say I am but a poor Suckling,
    And thus you cry me down.

Well, its no matter what you say
Of me or mine, that ran away ;
    I hold it no good fashion
A loyal subject's blood to spill,
When we have knaves enough to kill
    By force and proclamation.

Commend me unto Lashly[1] stout,
And all his pedlars him about :
    Tell them without remorse
That I will plunder all their packs
Which they have gotten, with the stolen
    knick-knacks,
    With these my hundred horse.

This holy war, this zealous firk,
Against the bishops and the kirk,
    And its pretended bravery—
Religion, all the world can tell,
Amongst Highlanders ne'er did dwell—
    Its but to cloak your knavery.

Such desperate gamesters as you be,
I cannot blame for tutoring me,
    Since all you have is down ;
And every boor forgets the plough,
And swears that he'll turn gamester now
    And venture for a crown.

---

[1] [Leslie, the hero of Newburn. The spelling *Lashly* is preserved, as it may have been intentionally so written.]

AGLAURA.

Aglaura. London, Printed by John Haviland for Thomas Walkley, and are to be sold at his shop . . . 1638. Folio.

⁎ The only edition printed in the author's lifetime.

Aglaura. Presented at the Private House in Black Fryers by His Majestie's servants. Written by Sir John Suckling.

This and the other dramas are printed in all the old copies with an utter disregard to punctuation, arrangement of lines, and other such details. The edition of 1658 corrects occasionally those of 1646-48, and *vice versâ.*

The neglect of metrical rules is so complete throughout, that a good deal of the dialogue in these productions is incapable of arrangement as verse.

Probably few books of the seventeenth century were more carelessly printed than Suckling's works. English typography was then in its lowest state of degradation.

PROLOGUE.

I'VE thought upon 't; and cannot tell which way
   Ought I can say now should advance the play;
For plays are either good or bad : the good,
If they do beg, beg to be understood;
And, in good faith, that has as bold a sound,
As if a beggar should ask twenty pound.
Men have it not about them:
Then, gentlemen, if rightly understood,
The bad do need less prologue than the good;
For, if it chance the plot be lame or blind,
Ill-clothed, deformed throughout, it needs must find
Compassion. It is a beggar without art,
But it falls out in pennyworths of wit,
As in all bargains else—men ever get
All they can in; will have London measure,
A handful over in their very pleasure.
And now ye have 't, he could not well deny 'e,
And I dare swear he's scarce a saver by ye.

THOSE common passions, hopes and fears, that
      still,
The poets first, and then the prologues fill,
In this our age : he that writ this, by me
Protests against as modest foolery.
He thinks it an odd thing to be in pain
For nothing else, but to be well again.
Who writes to fear is so : had he not writ,
You ne'er had been the judges of his wit ;
And when he had, did he but then intend
To please himself, he sure might have his end
Without the expense of hope ; and that he had,
That made this play, although the play be bad.
Then, gentlemen, be thrifty, save your dooms
For the next man or the next play that comes ;
For smiles are nothing where men do not care,
And frowns as little where they need not fear.

THIS, Sir, to them, but unto Majesty
    All he has said before he does deny.
Yet not to Majesty—that were to bring
His fears to be but for the Queen and King,
Not for yourselves; and that he dares not say
You are his sovereigns another way,
Your souls are princes, and you have as good
A title that way, as ye have by blood,
To govern; and here your power's more great
And absolute than in the royal seat.
There men dispute, and but by law obey,
Here is no law at all, but what ye say.

Dramatis Personæ.

KING, in love with Aglaura.

THERSAMES, Prince, in love with Aglaura.

ORBELLA, Queen, at first mistress to Ziriff; in love with Ariaspes.

ARIASPES, brother to the King.

ZIRIFF, otherwise Zorannes disguised, Captain of the Guard, in love with Orbella; brother to Aglaura.

IOLAS, a Lord of the Council, seeming friend to the Prince, but a traitor, in love with Semanthe.

AGLAURA, in love with the Prince, but named mistress to the King.

ORSAMES, a young lord anti-Platonic; friend to the Prince.

PHILAN, the same.

SEMANTHE, in love with Ziriff—Platonic.

ORITHIE, in love with Thersames.

PASITHAS, a faithful servant.

IOLINA, Aglaura's waiting-woman.

      Courtiers.   Huntsmen.   Priest.   Guard.

SCŒNA, PERSIA.

To Sir IOHN SUTLIN upon his

Aglaura : First, a bloody Tragedy, then by

the said Sir IOHN turn'd to a

COMEDY.[1]

WHEN first I read thy book, methought each
    word
Seem'd a short Dagger, and each line a Sword.
Where Women, Men ; Good, Bad ; Rich, Poore—all
    dy :
That needs must prove a fatal Tragedy.
But when I find, whom I so late saw slain
In thy first Book, in this revive again,
I cannot but with others much admire
In humane shape a more than earthly Fire.
So when Prometheus did inform this Clay,
He stole his Fire from heaven.   What shall I say ?
First for to Kill, and then to life restore,
This *Sutlin* did : the Gods can do no more.

.[1] These lines originally appeared at the end of the Elegy
on Suckling, 4to, 1642, inserted in the Appendix.

AGLAURA.

—✦—

ACTUS I. SCŒNA I.

Enter IOLAS, IOLINA.

Iol. MARRIED! and in Diana's grove!
    Iolin. So was th' appointment, or my
    sense deceived me.
  Iol. Married!
Now by those powers that tie those pretty knots,
Tis very fine: good faith, 'tis wondrous fine.
  Iolin. What is, brother?
  Iol. Why, to marry, sister;
T' enjoy 'twixt lawful and unlawful thus
A happiness, steal as it were his own;
Diana's grove, sayest thou?   [*Scratcheth his head.*
  Iolin. That is the place; the hunt once up, and all
Engaged in the sport, they mean to leave
The company, and steal unto those thickets,
Where there's a priest attends them.
  Iol. And will they lie together, think'st thou?
  Iolin. Is there distinction of sex, think you,
Or flesh and blood?
  Iol. True; but the king, sister!
  Iolin. But love, brother!
  Iol. Thou sayest well; 'tis fine, 'tis wondrous fine!
Diana's grove?
  Iolin. Yes, Diana's grove; but, brother,
If you should speak of this now.
  Iol.   Why, thou knowest

A drowning man holds not a thing so fast:
Semanthe!

> [*Enter Semanthe; she sees Iolas, and goes
> in again.*

She shuns me too!

Iolin. The wound festered sure:
The hurt the boy gave her, when first
She looked abroad into the world, is not yet cured.

Iol. What hurt?

Iolin. Why, know you not
She was in love long since with young Zorannes
(Aglaura's brother), and the now queen's betrothed?

Iol. Some such slight tale I've heard,

Iolin. Slight? she yet does weep, when she but
hears him named,
And tells the prettiest and the saddest stories
Of all those civil wars, and those amours,
That, trust me, both my lady and myself
Turn weeping statues still.

Iol. Pish! 'tis not that.
'Tis Ziriff and his fresh glories here
Have robbed me of her.
Since he thus appeared in court,
My love has languished worse than plants in drought.
But time's a good physician.　Come, let's in.
The king and queen by this time are come forth.

> [*Exeunt.*

Enter Serving-men *to* ZIRIFF.

1 *Serv.* Yonder's a crowd without, as if some
strange sight were to be seen to-day here.

2 *Serv.* Two or three with carbonadoes afore
instead of faces mistook the door for a breach,
and, at the opening of it, are striving still which
should enter first.

3 *Serv.* Is my lord busy?　　　　　　[*Knocks.*

Enter ZIRIFF, *as in his study.*

1 *Serv.* My lord, there are some soldiers without.

Zir. Well, I will despatch them presently.

2 *Serv.* The ambassadors from the Cadusians too.

Zir. Show them the gallery.

3 *Serv.* One from the king.

Zir. Again? I come, I come.

[*Exeunt Serving-men.*

ZIRIFF *solus.*

Greatness, thou vainer shadow of the prince's beams,
Begot by mere reflection, nourished in extremes;
First taught to creep, and live upon the glance,
Poorly to fare, till thine own proper strength
Bring thee to surfeit of thyself at last:
How dull a pageant would this states-play seem
To me now, were not my love and my revenge
Mix'd with it?
Three tedious winters have I waited here,
Like patient chemists blowing still the coals,
And still expecting, when the blessed hour
Would come, should make me master of
The Court Elixir Power; for that turns all.
'Tis in projection now; down, sorrow, down,
And swell my heart no more, and thou, wrong'd
    ghost
Of my dead father, to thy bed again,
And sleep securely!
It cannot be long, for sure fate must,
As it has been cruel, so [in] a while be just. [*Exit.*

Enter KING *and* Lords, *the* Lords *entreating for
    prisoners.*

King. I say they shall not live; our mercy
Would turn [to] sin, should we but use it e'er:
Pity and love the bosses only be
Of government merely for show and ornament.
Fear is the bit that man's proud will restrains,
And makes its vice its virtue. See it done.

Enter to them QUEEN, AGLAURA, Ladies. *The* KING
addresses himself to AGLAURA.

So early and so curious in your dress, fair mistress !
These pretty ambushes and traps for hearts,
Set with such care to-day, look like design :
Speak, lady, is't a massacre resolved ?
Is conquering one by one grown tedious sport ?
Or is the number of the taken such,
That for your safety you must kill outright ?

   Agl. Did none do greater mischief, sir, than I,
Heaven would not much be troubled with sad story,
Nor would the quarrel man has to the stars
Be kept alive so strongly.

   King. When he does leave it,
Women must take it up, and justly too ;
For robbing of the sex, and giving all to you.

   Agl. Their weaknesses you mean, and I confess,
     sir.

   King. The greatest subjects of their power or
     glory.
Such gentle rape thou act'st upon my soul,
And with such pleasing violence dost force it still,
That, when it should resist, it tamely yields,
Making a kind of haste to be undone,
As if the way to victory were loss,
And conquest came by overthrow.

   Enter an Express, *delivering a packet upon his knee.*
     The KING *reads.*

   Queen. Pretty ! [*The Queen, looking upon a flower*
     in one of the Ladies' heads.
Is it the child of nature, or of some fair hand ?

   La. 'Tis as the beauty, madam, of some faces,
Art's issue only.

   King. Thersames,
This concerns you most ; brought you her picture ?

   Exp. Something made up for her in haste I have.
     [*Presents the picture.*

King. If she does owe no part of this fair dower
Unto the painter, she is rich enough.

Agl. A kind of merry sadness in this face
Becomes it much.

King. There is indeed, Aglaura,
A pretty sullenness dress'd up in smiles,
That says this beauty can both kill and save.
How like you her, Thersames?

Ther. As well as any man can do a house
By seeing of the portal; here's but a face;
And faces, sir, are things I have not studied;
I have my duty, and may boldly swear,
What you like best will ever please me most.

King. Spoke like Thersames and my son!
Come: the day holds fair.
Let all the huntsmen meet us in the vale;
We will uncouple there.   [*Exeunt.*

ARIASPES *solus.*

Ari. How odd a thing a crowd is unto me!
Sure nature intended I should be alone.
Had not that old doting man-midwife Time
Slept when he should have brought me forth, I had
Been so to.   [*Studies and scratches his head.*
To be born near, and only near a crown!

Enter IOLAS.

Iol. How now, my lord?
What, walking o' th' tops of pyramids?
Whispering yourself away
Like a denied lover? come, to horse, to horse!
And I will show you straight a sight shall please
      you,
More than kind looks from her you dote upon
After a falling out.

Ari. Prithee, what is't?

Iol. I'll tell you as I go.   [*Exeunt.*

VOL. I.   G

Enter Huntsmen *hallooing and whooping.*

Hunts. Which way, which way?

Enter THERSAMES, *with* AGLAURA *muffled.*

Ther. This is the grove, 'tis somewhere here
within. [*Exeunt.*

Enter, dogging of them, ARIASPES, IOLAS.

Iol. Gently, gently!

Enter ORSAMES, PHILAN, *a* Huntsman, *two* Courtiers.

Hunts. No hurt, my lord, I hope?

Ors. None, none;
Thou wouldst have warranted it to another,
If I had broke my neck.
What! dost think my horse and I show tricks?
That which way soever he throws me,
Like a tumbler's boy I must fall safe?
Was there a bed of roses there? would I were eunuch,
if I had not as lief have fallen in the state as where
I did! the ground was as hard as if it had been
paved with Platonic ladies' hearts, and this uncon-
scionable fellow asks whether I have no hurt!
Where's my horse?

1 *Court.* Making love to the next mare, I think.

2 *Court.* Not the next, I assure you;
He 's gallop'd away, as if all the spurs i' th' field
Were in his sides.

Ors. Why, there it is: the jade's in the fashion
too.
Now he's done me an injury, he will not come
near me!
Well, when I hunt next, may I be upon a starv'd
cow,
Without a saddle too. And may I fall into a sawpit,
And not be taken up, but with suspicion

Of having been private with mine own beast there.
Now I better consider on't too, gentlemen,
'Tis but the same thing we do at court ;
Here's every man striving who shall be foremost,
    and
Hotly pursuing of what he seldom overtakes,
Or if he does, it's no great matter.

   Phi. He that's best hors'd, that is, best friended,
Gets in soonest, and then all he has to do
Is to laugh at those that are behind. Shall we
Help you, my lord ?

   Ors. Prithee, do. Stay !
To be in view's to be in favour, is it not ?

   Phi. Right.
And he that has a strong faction against him, hunts
upon a cold scent, and may in time come to a loss.

   Ors. Here's one rides two miles about, while
another leaps a ditch, and is in before him.

   Phi. Where note, the indirect way's the nearest !

   Ors. Good again !

   Phi. And here's another puts on, and falls into a
quagmire, that is, follows the court, till he has spent
all ; for your court quagmire is want of money—
there a man is sure to stick, and then not one helps
him out, if they do not laugh at him.

   1 *Court.* What think you of him that hunts after
    my rate,
And never sees the deer ?

   2 *Court.* Why, he is like some young fellow that
    follows
The court and never sees the king.

   Ors. To spur a horse, till he is tired, is——

   Phi. To importune a friend till he weary of you.

   Ors. For then, upon the first occasion, you're
    thrown off,
As I was now.

   Phi. This is nothing to the catching of your horse,
    Orsames.

Ors. Thou sayest true : I think he is no transmi-
  grated
Philosopher, .and therefore not likely to be taken
  with mortals.
Gentlemen, your help ; the next, I hope, will be
  yours,
And then 'twill be my turn.   *[Exeunt.*

Enter again, married, THERSAMES *and* AGLAURA,
  with Priest.

Ther. Fear not, my dear ; if, when love's diet
Was bare looks, and those stol'n too,
He yet did thrive, what then
Will he do now ? when every night must be
A feast, and every day fresh revelry !
  Ang. Will he not surfeit when he once shall come
To grosser fare, my lord, and so grow sick ?
And love once sick, how quickly it will die !
  Ther. Ours cannot ; 'tis as immortal as the things
That elemented it, which were our souls :
Nor can they e'er impair in health, for what
These holy rites do warrant us to do,
More than our bodies would for quenching thirst.
Come, let's to horse ; we shall be miss'd ;
For we are envy's mark, and court eyes carry far.
Your prayers and silence, sir.   *[To the Priest.*
                                 [Exeunt.

Enter ARIASPES, IOLAS.

Ari. If it succeed, I wear thee here, my Iolas.
  Iol. If it succeed ? will night succeed the day,
Or hours one to another ? is not his lust
The idol of his soul, and was not she
The idol of his lust ? As safely he might
Have stol'n the diadem from off his head,
And he would less have miss'd it.
You now, my lord, must raise his jealousy :
Teach it to look through the false optic, fear,

And make it see all double.   Tell him, the prince
Would not have thus presumed, but that he does
Intend worse yet ; and that his crown and life
Will be the next attempt.

   Ari. Right, and I will urge,
How dangerous it is unto the present state
To have the creatures and the followers
Of the next prince, whom all now strive to please,
Too near about him.

   Iol. What, if the malcontents, that use
To come unto him, were discovered ?

   Ari. By no means ; for it were in vain to give
Him discontent (which, too, must needs be done),
If they within him gave it not nourishment.

   Iol. Well, I'll away first, for the print's too big,
If we be seen together.   [*Exit.*

   Ari. I have so fraught this bark with hope, that it
Dares venture now in any storm or weather ;
And if he sinks or splits, all's one to me.
" Ambition seems all things, and yet is none,
But in disguise stalks to opinion,
And fools it into faith for everything."
'Tis not with the ascending to a throne
As 'tis with stairs and steps that are the same ;
For to a crown each humour's a degree ;
And as men change and differ, so must we.
The name of virtue doth the people please,
Not for their love to virtue, but their ease.
And parrot-rumour I that tale have taught,
By making love I hold the woman's grace ;
'Tis the court's double key, and entrance gets
To all the little plots.   The fiery spirits
My love to arms hath drawn into my faction ;
All but the minion of the time is mine,
And he shall be, or shall not be at all.
He that beholds a wing in pieces torn,
And knows not that to heav'n it once did bear
The high-flown and self-lessening bird, will think

And call them idle subjects of the wind :
When he that has the skill to imp and bind
These in right places, will this truth discover,
That borrowed instruments do oft convey
The soul to her propos'd intents, and where
Our stars deny, art may supply.　　　　　*[Exit.*

　　Enter SEMANTHE, ORITHIE, ORSAMES, PHILAN.

　　Sem. Think you it is not then
The little jealousies, my lord, and fears :
Joy mix'd with doubt, and doubt reviv'd with hope,
That crowns all love with pleasure? these are lost,
When once we come to full fruition :
Like waking in the morning, when all night
Our fancy has been fed with some new strange
　　delight.
　　Ors. I grant you, madam, that the fears and joys,
Hopes and desires, mix'd with despairs and doubts,
Do make the sport in love ; [and] that they are
The very dogs by which we hunt the hare ;
But as the dogs would stop, and straight give o'er,
Were it not for the little thing before ;
So would our passions ; both alike must be
Flesh'd in the chase.
　　Ori. Will you, then, place the happiness but there,
Where the dull ploughman and the ploughman's
　　horse
Can find it out? Shall souls refin'd not know
How to preserve alive a noble flame,
But let it die—burn out to appetite?
　　Sem. Love's a chameleon, and would live on air,
Physic for agues ; starving is his food.
　　Ors. Why, there it is now ! a greater epicure
Lives not on earth. My lord and I have been
In's privy kitchen, seen his bills of fare.
　　Sem. And how, and how, my lord?
　　Ors. A mighty prince, and full of curiosity !
Hearts newly slain serv'd up entire,

And stuck with little arrows instead of cloves.

Phi. Sometimes a cheek plump'd up
With broth, with cream and claret mingled
For sauce, and round about the dish
Pomegranate kernels, strew'd on leaves of lilies!

Ors. Then will he have black eyes, for those of
late
He feeds on much, and for variety the grey.

Phi. You forget his cover'd dishes
Of jenestrays, and marmalade of lips,
Perfum'd by breath sweet as the bean's first blossoms.

Sem. Rare!
And what's the drink to all this meat, my lord?

Ors. Nothing but pearl dissolv'd, tears still fresh
fetch'd
From lovers' eyes, which, if they come to be
Warm in the carriage, are straight cool'd with sighs.

Sem. And all this rich proportion perchance
We would allow him:

Ors. True! but therefore this is but his common
diet:
Only serves when his chief cooks,
Liking and Opportunity, are out of the way.
For when he feasts indeed,
'Tis there where the wise people of the world
Did place the virtues—i' th' middle, madam.

Ori. My lord, there is so little hope we should
convert you;
And if we should, so little got by it,
That we'll not lose so much upon't as sleep.
Your lordship's servants.   [*Prepare to go.*

Ors. Nay, ladies, we will wait upon you to your
chambers.

Phi. Prithee, let's spare the compliment, we shall
Do no good.

Ors.   By this hand, I'll try;
They keep me fasting, and I must be praying.
                                          [*Exeunt.*

AGLAURA *undressing herself.* IOLINA.

Agl. Undress me; is it not late, Iolina?
It was the longest day this——

Enter THERSAMES.

Ther. Softly, as death itself comes on,
When it does steal away the sick man's breath,
And standers-by perceive it not,
Have I trod the way unto these lodgings.
How wisely do those powers
That give us happiness, order it!
Sending us still fears to bound our joys,
Which else would overflow and lose themselves:
See where she sits,
Like day retir'd into another world.
Dear mine! where all the beauty man admires
In scattered pieces does united lie.
Where sense does feast, and yet where sweet desire
Lives in its longing, like a miser's eye,
That never knew nor saw satiety:
Tell me, by what approaches must I come
To take in what remains of my felicity?
Agl. Needs there any new ones, where the breach
Is made already? you are enter'd here,
Long since, sir, here, and I have giv'n up all.
Ther. All but the fort; and in such wars as these,
Till that be yielded up, there is no peace
Nor triumph to be made. Come, undo, undo;
And from these envious clouds slide quick
Into love's proper sphere, thy bed.
The weary traveller, whom the busy sun
Hath vex'd all day, and scorch'd almost to tinder,
Ne'er long'd for night as I have long'd for this.
What rude hand is that?

      [*One knocks hastily. Iolina goes to the door.*
Go, Iolina, see, but let none enter——

Iolin. 'Tis Ziriff, sir.

Ther. O, something of weight hath fallen out, it seems,

Which in his zeal he could not keep till morning.

But one short minute, dear, into that chamber.

[Exit Aglaura.

Enter ZIRIFF.

How now? thou start'st as if thy sins had met thee,

Or thy father's ghost; what news, man?

Zir. Such as will send the blood of hasty messages

Unto the heart, and make it call

All that is man about you into council:

Where is the princess, sir?

Ther. Why, what of her?

Zir. The king must have her.

Ther. How?

Zir. The king must have her, sir.

Ther. Though fear of worse makes ill still relish better;

And this look handsome in our friendship, Ziriff,

Yet so severe a preparation

There needed not. Come, come, what is't?

      [Ziriff leads him to the door, and shows him a

A guard!   *guard.*

Thersames, thou art lost; betray'd

By faithless and ungrateful man, out of a happiness.

      [He steps between the door and him, and draws.

The very thought of that

Will lend my anger so much noble justice

That, wert thou master of as much fresh life

As thou'st been of villainy, it should not serve

Nor stock thee out to glory or repent

The least of it.

Zir. Put up, put up! such unbecoming anger

I have not seen you wear before.

What, draw upon your friend!   *[Discovers himself.*

Do you believe me right now?

Ther. I scarce believe mine eyes! Zorannes?

Zir. The same, but how preserv'd, or why
Thus long disguis'd, to you a freer hour must speak.
That you're betray'd, is certain; but by whom,
Unless the priest himself, I cannot guess,
More than the marriage though he knows not of.
If you now send her on this early summons,
Before the sparks are grown into a flame,
You do redeem th' offence, or make it less;
And, on my life, his intents are fair,
And he will but besiege, not force affection.
So you gain time. If you refuse, there's but
One way; you know his power and passion.

Ther. Into how strange a labyrinth am I
Now fall'n! what shall I do, Zorannes?

Zir. Do, sir, as seamen that have lost their light
And way: strike sail, and lie quiet a while.
Your forces in the province are not yet
In readiness, nor is our friend Zephines
Arriv'd at Delphos; nothing is ripe. Besides——

Ther. Good heavens! did I but dream that she
was mine?
Upon imagination did I climb up to
This height? Let me then wake and die:
Some courteous hand snatch me from what's to come,
And, ere my wrongs have being, give them end.

Zir. How poor and how unlike the prince is this!
This trifle woman does unman us all:
Robs us so much. it makes us things of pity.
Is this a time to lose our anger in,
And vainly breathe it out, when all we have
Will hardly fill the sail of Resolution,
And make us bear up high enough for action?

Ther. I have done, sir; pray chide no more;
The slave, whom tedious custom has inur'd,
And taught to think of misery as of food,
Counting it but a necessary of life,
And so digesting it, shall not so much as once

Be nam'd to patience, when I am spoken of.
Mark me ; for I will now undo myself
As willingly as virgins all give up
First nights to them they love.   [*Offers to go out.*

   Zir. Stay, sir, 'twere fit Aglaura yet were kept
In ignorance.   I will dismiss the guard,
And be myself again.   [*Exit.*

   Ther.   In how much worse estate am I in now,
Than if I ne'er had known her !   Privation
Is a misery as much above bare wretchedness
As that is short of happiness :
So when the sun does not appear,
'Tis darker, 'cause it once was here.

      Enter Ziriff, *speaks to* Orsames *and others half
entered.*

   Zir. Nay, gentlemen,
There needs no force where there is no resistance :
I'll satisfy the king myself.

   Ther.   O, it is well ye are come.
There was within me fresh rebellion,
And reason was almost unking'd again.
But you shall have her, sir.

         [*Goes out to fetch Aglaura.*

   Zir. What doubtful combats in this noble youth
Passion and reason have !

      Enter Thersames, *leading* Aglaura.

   Ther. Here, sir.   [*Gives her and goes out.*
   Agl. What means the prince, my lord ?
   Zir. Madam, his wiser fear has taught him to dis-
    guise
His love, and make it look a little rude at parting.
Affairs, that do concern all that you hope
From happiness, this night force him away ;
And lest you should have tempted him to stay,
Which he did doubt you would, and would prevail—

He left you thus ; he does desire by me
Yon would this night lodge in the little tower,
Which is in my command ; the reasons why
Himself will shortly tell you.

   Agl. 'Tis strange, but I am all obedience. [*Exeunt.*

ACTUS II. SCŒNA I.

Enter THERSAMES, *with* IOLAS, *a Lord of the Council.*

   Iol. I told him, sir ; urg'd 'twas no common knot,
That to the tying of it two powerful princes,
Virtue and Love, were join'd, and that a greater
Than these two was now engaged in't, Religion.
But 'twould not do ; the cork of passion
Buoy'd up all reason so, that what was said
Swam but o' th' top of th' ear, ne'er reach'd the
    heart.

   Ther. Is there no way for kings to show their
    power
But in their subjects' wrongs ? no subject neither,
But his own son ?

   Iol. Right, sir :
No quarry for his lust to gorge on, but on what
You fairly had flown at and taken ?
Well, were it not the king, or were't indeed
Not you, that have such hopes, and such a crown
To venture, and yet it is but a woman.

   Ther. How ? that *but* again ! and thou art more
    injurious
Than he, and wouldst provoke me sooner !

   Iol. Why, sir ?
There are no altars yet address'd unto her,
Nor sacrifice. If I have made her less
Than what she is, it was my love to you ;
For in my thoughts and here within I hold her
The noblest piece Nature e'er lent our eyes,
And of the which all women else are but

Weak counterfeits, made up by her journeymen :
But was this fit to tell you?
I know you value but too high all that.
And in a loss we should not make things more ;
'Tis misery's happiness that we can make it less
By art, through a forgetfulness upon
Our ills. Yet who can do it here?
When every voice must needs, and' every face,
Showing what she was not, show what she was.

    Ther. I'll instantly upon him.   [*Draws.*

    Iol. Stay, sir.
Though't be the utmost of my fortune's hope
To have an equal share of ill with you :
Yet I could wish we sold this trifle life
At a far dearer rate than we are like to do,
Since 'tis a king's the merchant.

    Ther. Ha !
King? Ay, it is indeed ;
And there's no art can cancel that high bond.

    Iol. He cools again.   [*To himself.*
True, sir, and yet methinks to know a reason :
For passive nature ne'er had glorious end ;
And he that states' preventions ever learn'd,
Knows 'tis one motion to strike and to defend.

Enter Serving-man.

    Serv. Some of the lords without, and from the king,
They say, wait you.

    Ther. What subtle state-trick now?
But one turn here, and I am back, my lord.   [*Exit.*

    Iol. This will not do ; his resolution's like
A skilful horseman, and reason is the stirrup,
Which, though a sudden shock may make
It loose, yet does it meet it handsomely again.
Stay, it must be some sudden fear of wrong
To her, that may draw on a sudden act
From him, and ruin from the king ; for such
A spirit will not, like common ones, be

Raised by every spell; 'tis in love's circle
Only it will appear.

Enter THERSAMES.

Ther. I cannot bear the burthen of my wrongs
One minute longer.

Iol. Why! what's the matter, sir?

Ther. They do pretend the safety of the state:
Now, nothing but my marriage with Cadusia
Can secure the adjoining country to it;
Confinement during life for me if I refuse.
Diana's nunnery for her; and at that nunn'ry, Iolas,
Allegiance in me, like the string of a watch
Wound up too high, and forc'd above the nick,
Ran back, and in a moment was unravell'd all.

Iol. Now, by the love I bear to justice,
That nunn'ry was too severe.   When virtuous love's
    a crime,
What man can hope to 'scape a punishment,
Or who's indeed so wretched to desire it?

Ther. Right!

Iol. What answer made you, sir?

Ther. None: they gave me till to-morrow,
And e'er that be, or they or I
Must know our destiny.
Come, friend, let's in; there is no sleeping now;
For time is short, and we have much to do. [*Exeunt.*

Enter ORSAMES, PHILAN, Courtiers.

Ors. Judge you, gentlemen, if I be not as unfor-
    tunate
As a gamester thinks himself upon the loss
Of the last stake; this is the first she
I ever swore to heartily, and, by those eyes,
I think I had continued unperjur'd a whole month,
And that's fair, you'll say.

1 Court. Very fair.

Ors. Had she not run mad betwixt!

2 *Court.* How? mad?

Who? Semanthe?

  Ors. Yea, yea, mad; ask Philan else.

People that want clear intervals talk not

So wildly. I'll tell you, gallants; 'tis now, since first I

Found myself a little hot and quivering 'bout the heart,

Some ten days since; a tedious ague, sirs:

But what of that?

The gracious glance and little whisper pass'd,

Approaches made from th' hand unto the lip,

I came to visit her, and as, you know, we use

Breathing a sigh or two by the way of prologue,

Told her in love's physic 'twas a rule,

Where the disease had birth, to seek a cure.

I had no sooner nam'd love to her, but she

Began to talk of flames, and flames

Neither devouring nor devour'd, of air

And of chameleons.

  1 *Court.* O the Platonics!

  2 *Court.* Those of the new religion in love! your lordship's merry,

Troth, how do you like the humour on't?

  Ors. As thou wouldst like red hair or leanness

In thy mistress, scurvily! 't does worse with hand-someness

Than strong desire could do with impotence:

A mere trick to enhance the price of kisses.

  Phi. Surely these silly women, when they feed

Our expectation so high, do but like

Ignorant conjurers, that raise a spirit,

Which handsomely they cannot lay again.

  Ors. True, 'tis like some that nourish up

Young lions, till they grow so great they are afraid of

Themselves: they dare not grant at last,

For fear they should not satisfy.

  Phi. Who's for the town? I must take up again.

Ors. This villainous love's as changeable as the
philosopher's stone, and thy mistress as hard to
compass too!

Phi. The Platonic is ever so; they are as tedious,
Before they come to the point, as an old man
Fall'n into the stories of his youth.

2 *Court.* Or a widow into the praises of her first
husband.

Ors. Well, if she hold out but one month longer,
If I do not quite forget I e'er beleaguered there,
And remove the siege to another place, may all
The curses beguil'd virgins loose upon
Their perjur'd lovers fall upon me.

Phi. And thou wouldst deserve 'em all.

Ors. For what?

Phi. For being in the company of those
That took away the prince's mistress from him.

Ors. Peace, that will be redeem'd.
I put but on this wildness to disguise myself;
There are brave things in hand, hark i' thy ear.

[*Whispers.*

1 *Court.* Some severe plot upon a maidenhead.
These two young lords make love,
As embroiderers work against a masque, night and
day;
They think importunity a nearer way than merit,
And take women as schoolboys catch squirrels;
Hunt 'em up and down, till they are weary,
And fall down before 'em.

Ors. Who loves the prince fails not——

Phi. And I am one: my injuries are great as
thine,
And do persuade as strongly.

Ors. I had command to bring thee;
Fail not, and in thine one disguise.

Phi. Why in disguise?

Ors. It is the prince's policy and love;
For, if we should miscarry,

Some one taken might betray the rest,
Unknown to one another;
Each man is safe in his own valour.

    2 *Court.* And what mercer's wife are you to
      cheapen now
Instead of his silks?

    Ors. Troth; 'tis not so well; 'tis but a cousin of
      thine:
Come, Philan, let's along.   *[Exeunt.*

Enter QUEEN alone.

    Orb. What is it thus within whispering remorse,
And calls love tyrant? all powers but his
Their rigour and our fear have made divine.
But every creature holds of him by sense—
The sweetest tenure. Ye're but my husband's
    brother:
And what of that? do harmless birds or beasts
Ask leave of curious Heraldry at all?
Does not the womb of one fair spring
Bring unto the earth many sweet rivers,
That wantonly do one another chase,
And in one bed kiss, mingle, and embrace?
Man (Nature's heir) is not by her will tied,
To shun all creatures are allied unto him,
For then she should shun all; since death and life
Doubly allies all them that live by breath:
The air that doth impart to all life's brood
Refreshment, is so near to itself, and to us all,
That all in all is individual.
But how am I sure one and the same desire
Warms Ariaspes; for art can keep alive
A bedrid love?

Enter ARIASPES.

    Ari. Alone, madam, and overcast with thought!
Uncloud, uncloud; for, if we may believe
The smiles of fortune, love shall no longer pine

In prison thus, nor undelivered travail
With throes of fear and of desire about it.
The prince, like to a valiant beast in nets,
Striving to force a freedom suddenly,
Has made himself at length the surer prey:
The king stands only now betwixt, and is
Just like a single tree, that hinders all the prospect:
'Tis but the cutting down of him, and we——

   Orb. Why, wouldst thou thus embark into strange
      seas,
And trouble Fate for what we have already?
Thou art to me, what thou now seek'st, a kingdom;
And were thy love as great as thy ambition,
I should be so to thee.

   Ari. Think you you are not, madam?
As well and justly may you doubt the truths
Tortur'd or dying men do leave behind them:
But then my fortune turns my misery,
When my addition shall but make you less;
Shall I endure that head, that wore a crown,
For my sake should wear none? First, let me
      lose
Th' exchequer of my wealth—your love; nay, may
All that rich treasury you have about you,
Be rifled by the man I hated, and I look on;
Though youth be full of sin, and heaven be just,
So sad a doom I hope they keep not for me;
Remember what a quick apostasy he made,
When all his vows were up to heav'n and you.
How, ere the bridal torches were burnt out,
His flames grew weak and sicklier: think on that.
Think how unsafe you are, if she should now
Not sell her honour at a lower rate
Than your place in his bed.

    Orb. And would not you prove false, too, then?
    Ari. By this—and this—love's breakfast;
                           [*Kisses her.*
By his feasts, too, yet to come, by all the

Beauty in this face, divinity too great
To be profan'd !
   Orb. O, do not swear by that;
Cankers may eat that flower upon the stalk
(For sickness and mischance are great devourers),
And when there is not in these cheeks and lips
Left red enough to blush at perjury,
When you shall make it, what shall I do then ?
   Ari. Our souls by that time, madam,
Will by long custom so acquainted be,
They will not need that duller trouch-man Flesh,
But freely, and without those poorer helps,
Converse and mingle ; meantime we will teach
Our loves to speak, not thus to live by signs,
And action is his native language, madam.

Enter ZIRIFF *unseen.*

This box but open'd to the sense will do it.
   Orb. I undertake, I know not what.
   Ari. Thine own safety, dearest.
Let it be this night, if thou dost
Love thyself or me.   [*Whisper and kiss.*
   Orb. That's very sudden.
   Ari. Not, if we be so, and we must now be wise,
For when their sun sets, ours begins to rise. [*Exeunt.*

ZIRIFF *solus.*

   Zir. Then all my fears are true, and she is false ;
False as a falling star or glowworm's fire.
This devil Beauty is compounded strangely :
It is a subtle point, and hard to know,
Whether 't has in't more active tempting,
Or [is] more passive tempted ; so soon it forces,
And so soon it yields.
Good Gods ! she seiz'd my heart, as if from you
She'd had commission to have us'd me so ;
And all mankind besides. And see, if the
Just ocean makes more haste to pay

To needy rivers, what is borrow'd first,
Than she to give, where she ne'er took.
Methinks I feel anger, revenge's harbinger,
Chalking up all within, and thrusting out
Of doors the tame and softer passions.
It must be so :
To love is noble frailty, but poor sin,
When we fall once to love, [to be] unloved again.

[*Exit*

Enter KING, ARIASPES, IOLAS.

Ari. 'Twere fit your justice did consider, sir,
What way it took.   If you should apprehend
The prince for treason, which he never did,
And which (unacted) is unborn—at least 'twill be
believ'd so :
Lookers-on and the loud-talking crowd
Will think it all but water-colours laid
On for a time ; and which, wiped off, each common
eye
Would see strange ends through stranger ways.
    King. Think'st thou I will compound with treason
then ?
And make one fear another's advocate ?
    Iol. Virtue forbid, sir, but if you'd permit
Them to approach the room (yet who'd advise
Treason should come so near ?) there would be then
No place left for excuse.
    King. How strong are they ?
    Iol. Weak, considering
The enterprise ; they are but few in number,
And those few, too, having nothing but
Their resolutions considerable about them :
A troop indeed design'd to suffer what
They come to execute.
    King. Who are they are thus weary of their lives ?
    Iol. Their names I cannot give you.
For those he sent for, he did still receive

At a back door, and so dismiss'd them to.
But I do think Ziriff is one.

   King. Take heed! I shall suspect thy hate to
     others,
Not thy love to me, begot this service;
This treason, thou thyself dost say
Has but an hour's age, and I can give accompt
Of him beyond that time. Brother, in the little tower,
Where now Aglaura's prisoner,
You shall find him; bring him along.
He yet doth stand untainted in my thoughts,
Aud to preserve him so,
He shall not stir out of my eyes' command,
Till this great cloud be over.

   Iol. Sir, 'twas the prince, who first——
   King. I know all that! urge it no more!
I love the man;
And 'tis with pain we do suspect,
Where we do not dislike.
Thou'rt sure he will have some,
And that they will come to-night?

   Iol. As sure as night will come itself.
   King. Get all yonr guards in readiness; we will
     ourself
Disperse them afterwards; and both be sure
To wear your thoughts within: I'll act the rest.

                          [*Exeunt.*

    Enter PHILAN, ORSAMES, Courtiers.

   2 *Court.* Well, if there be not some great storm
     towards,
Ne'er trust me; Whisper (Court-thunder) is in
Every corner, and there has been to-day
About the town a murmuring
And buzzing, such as men use to make
When they do fear to vent their fears.

   1 *Court.* True, and all the statesmen hang down
     their heads,

Like full-ear'd corn ; two of them,
Where I supp'd, ask'd what time of night it was,
And when 'twas told them, started, as if
They had been to run a race.

    2 Court. The king, too, (if you mark him), doth
      feign mirth
And jollity ; but, through them both,
Flashes of discontent and anger make escapes.

    Ors. Gentlemen ! 'tis pity heav'n
Design'd you not to make the almanacs.
You guess so shrewdly by the ill aspects,
Or near conjunctions of the great ones,
At what's to come still, that without all doubt
The country had been govern'd wholly by you,
And plough'd and reap'd accordingly. For me,
I understand this mystery as little
As the new love ;[1] and as I take it, too,
'Tis much about the time that everything
But owls and lovers take their rest ;
Good-night, Philan. Away.   *[Exit.*

    1 Court. 'Tis early yet ; let's go on the queen's
      side,
And fool a little ; I love to warm myself,
Before I go to bed ; it does beget
Handsome and sprightly thoughts, and makes
Our dreams half-solid pleasures.

    2 Court. Agreed.   *[Exeunt.*

ACTUS III. SCŒNA I.

Enter PRINCE, Conspirators.

Ther. Couldst thou not find out Ziriff ?
    1 Court. Not speak with him, my lord,
Yet I sent in by several men.
    Ors. I wonder Iolas meets us not here, too.
    Ther. 'Tis strange, but let's on now howe'er ;

           [1] [Platonism.]

When fortunes, honour, life, and all's in doubt,
Bravely to dare is bravely to get out.
                        [The Guard upon them.

Ther. Betray'd! betray'd!   *[Excursions.*
Ors. Shift for yourself, sir, and let us alone;
We will secure your way, and make our own.
                               [Exeunt.

          Enter the KING *and* Lords.

King. Follow, lords, and see quick execution done;
Leave not a man alive.
Who treads on fire, and does not put it out,
Disperses fear in many sparks of doubt.   *[Exeunt.*

     Enter Conspirators, *and the* Guard *upon them.*

Ors. Stand, friends: an equal party.
    [Fight.] *Three of the Conspirators fall, and*
         three of the King's side: Orsames and
         Philan kill the rest. They throw off
         their disguises.
Phi. Brave Orsames, 'tis pleasure to die near thee.
Ors. Talk not of dying, Philan; we will live,
And serve the noble prince again: we are alone.
Off then with thy disguise, and throw it in the
    bushes.
Quick, quick! before the torrent comes upon us.
We shall be straight good subjects, and I despair not
Of reward for this night's service. So
We two now kill'd our friends! 'tis hard,
But 't must be so.

     Enter ARIASPES, IOLAS, *two* Courtiers, *part*
           of the Guard.

Ari. Follow, follow!
Ors. Yes, so you may now; ye're not likely to
    overtake.
Iol. Orsames and Philan! how came you hither?

Ors. The nearest way, it seems; you follow'd,
    thank you,
As if it had been through quicksets.
    Iol. 'Sdeath, have they all escap'd?
    Ors. Not all, two of them we made sure;
But they cost dear: look here else.
    Ari. Is the prince there?
    Phi. They are both princes, I think.
They fought like princes, I am sure.

> [*Iolas pulls off the vizors.*

    Iol. Stephines and Odiris.   We trifle.
Which way took the rest?
    Ors. Two of them are certainly hereabouts.
    Ari. Upon my life, they swam the river;
Come,[1] straight to horse, and follow o'er the bridge;
You and I, my lord, will search this place a little
    better.
    Ors. Your highness will, I hope, remember who
    were
The men were in——
    Ari. O, fear not, your mistress shall know ye're
    valiant.
    Ors. Philan, if thou lov'st me, let's kill them upon
    the place.
    Phi. Fie! thou now art wild indeed!
Thou taught'st me to be wise first,
And I will now keep thee so.   Follow, follow.

> [*Exeunt.*

Enter AGLAURA *with a lute.*

The Prince comes and knocks within.

    Ther. Madam!
    Agl. What wretch is this that thus usurps
Upon the privilege of ghosts, and walks
At midnight?
    Ther. Aglaura!

---

[1] [Old copies, *some.*]

Agl. Betray me not,
My willing sense, too soon; yet, if that voice
Be false.

Ther. Open, fair saint, and let me in.

Agl. It is the prince——
As willingly as those,
That cannot sleep do light; welcome, sir.   [*Opens.*
Welcome above.
Bless me, what means this unsheath'd minister of
      death?   [*Spies his sword drawn.*
If, sir, on me quick justice be to pass,
Why this? Absence, alas! or such strange looks
As you now bring with you, would kill as soon.

Ther. Softly! for I, like a hard-hunted deer,
Have only herded here; and though the cry
Reach not our ears, yet am I followed close:
O my heart! since I saw thee
Time has been strangely active, and begot
A monstrous issue of unheard-of story:
Sit; thou shalt have it all! nay, sigh not.
Such blasts will hinder all the passage;
Dost thou remember how we parted last?

Agl. Can I forget it, sir?

Ther. That word of parting was ill-plac'd, I swear.
It may be ominous; but dost thou know
Into whose hands I gave thee?

Agl. Yes, into Ziriff's, sir.

Ther. That Ziriff was thy brother, brave Zorannes,
Preserv'd by miracle in that sad day
Thy father fell, and since thus in disguise
Waiting his just revenge.

Agl. You do amaze me, sir.

Ther. And must do more, when I tell all the
      story.
The king, the jealous king, knew of the marriage,
And when thou thought'st thyself by my direction,
Thou wert his prisoner.
Unless I would renounce all right,

And cease to love thee—O strange and fond re-
　　quest!—
Immur'd thou must have been in some sad place,
And lock'd for ever from Thersame's sight,
For ever, and that unable to endure!
This night I did attempt his life.

　　Agl. Was it well done, sir?
　　Ther. O no! extremely ill!
For to attempt and not to act was poor.
Here the dead-doing law (like ill-paid soldiers)
Leaves the side it was on to join with power.
Royal villainy now will look so like to justice,
That the times to come and curious posterity
Will find no difference.　Weep'st thou, Aglaura?
Come to bed, my love!
And we will there mock tyranny and fate.
Those softer hours of pleasure and delight
That, like so many single hearts, should have
Adorn'd our thread of life, we will at once,
By love's mysterious power and this night's help,
Contract to one, and make but one rich draught
Of all.

　　Agl. What mean you, sir?
　　Ther. To make myself incapable of misery,
By taking strong preservatives of happiness:
I would this night enjoy thee.

　　Agl. Do, sir, do what you will with me;
For I am too much yours to deny the right
However claim'd; but——

　　Ther. But what, Aglaura?
　　Agl. Gather not roses in a wet and frowning hour,
They'll lose their sweets then, trust me they will, sir.
What pleasure can love take to play his game out,
When death must keep the stakes? [*A noise without.*
Hark, sir, grave-bringers and last minutes are at hand,
Hide, hide yourself; for love's sake, hide yourself!

　　Ther. As soon the sun may hide himself as I.
The Prince of Persia hide himself!

Agl. O, talk not, sir; the sun does hide himself,
When night and blackness comes.
 Ther Never, sweet ignorance, he shines in th'
  other world then ;
And so shall I, if I set here in glory.
Enter, ye hasty seekers of life.
      [Opens the door. Enter Ziriff.
Zorannes !
 Agl. My brother !
If all the joy within me come not out,
To give a welcome to so dear an object,
Excuse it, sir; sorrow locks up all doors.
 Zir. If there be such a toy about you, sister,
Keep 't for yourself, or lend it to the prince ;
There is a dearth of that commodity,
And you have made it, sir. Now,
What is the next mad thing you mean to do ?
Will you stay here ? when all the court's beset,
Like to a wood at a great hunt, and busy mischief
  hates
To be in view, and have you in her power——
 Ther. To me all this ?
For great grief's deaf, as well as it is dumb,
And drives no trade at all with counsel. Sir,
Why do you not tutor one that has the plague ,
And see if he will fear an after-ague fit ;
Such is all mischief now to me, there is none left
Is worth a thought ; death is the worst I know,
And that, compar'd to shame, does look more lovely
  now
Than a chaste mistress, set by a common woman ;
And I must court it, sir ?
 Zir. No wonder, if that heav'n
Forsake us when we leave ourselves :
What is there done should feed such high despair ?
Were you but safe——
 Agl. Dear sir, be rul'd ;
If love be love, and magic too,

As sure it is, where it is true;
We then shall meet in absence, and in spite
Of all divorce freely enjoy together
What niggard fate thus peevishly denies.

Ther. Yea : but, if pleasures be themselves but
    dreams,
What then are the dreams of these to men ?
That monster, Expectation, will devour
All that is within our hope or power,
And ere we once can come to show how rich
We are, we shall be poor,
Shall we not, Zorannes ?

Zir. I understand not this.
In times of envious penury, such as these are,
To keep but love alive is fair ; we should not think
Of feasting him. Come, sir :
Here in these lodgings is a little door,
That leads unto another ; that again
Unto a vault that has his passage under
The little river, opening into the wood ;
From thence 'tis but some few minutes' easy business
Unto a servant's house of mine, who for his faith
And honesty hereafter must
Look big in story. There you are safe, however ;
And when this storm has met a little calm,
What wild desire dares whisper to itself,
You may enjoy, and at the worst may steal.

Ther. What shall become of thee, Aglaura, then ?
Shall I leave thee their rage's sacrifice ?
And, like dull seamen threaten'd with a storm,
Throw all away I have to save myself ?

Agl. Can I be safe, when you are not, my lord ?
Knows love in us divided happiness ?
Am I the safer for your being here ?
Can you give that you have not for yourself ?
My innocence is my best guard, and that your stay,
Betraying it unto suspicion, takes away.
If you did love me——

Ther. Grows that in question? [*kisses her*] then
   'tis time to part!
When we shall meet again, heaven only knows;
And when we·shall, I know we shall be old.
Love does not calculate the common way;
Minutes are hours there, and the hours are days;
Each day's an year, and every year an age.
What will this come to, think you?
   Zir. Would this were all the ill!
For these are petty little harmless nothings.
Time's horse runs full as fast hard-borne and curb'd,
As in his full career, loose rein'd and spurr'd.
Come, come, let's av ay.
   Ther. Happiness such as men, lost in misery,
Would wrong in naming, 'tis so much above them.
All that I want of it, all you deserve,
Heaven send you in my absence!
   Agl. And misery such as witty malice would
Lay out in curses on the thing it hates,
Heaven send me in the stead, if when you are gone
     [*Leads him out, and enters up one of the vaults.*
I welcome it but for your sake alone.   [*Exeunt.*
   Zir. Stir not from hence, sir, till you hear from me,
So, good-night, dear prince.
   Ther. Good-night, dear friend.
   Zir. When we meet next, all this will but advance.
Joy never feasts so high,
As when the first course is of misery.   [*Exeunt.*

ACTUS IV. SCŒNA I.

Enter three or four Courtiers.

   1 *Court.* By this light, a brave prince!
He made no more of the guard, than they
Would of a tailor on a masque night, that has refused
Trusting before.
   2 *Court.* He's as active as he is valiant too?
Didst mark him how he stood like all the points

O' th' compass, and, as good pictures,
Had his eyes towards every man?[1]
   3 *Court.* And his sword too.
All th' other side walk up and down the court now
As if they had lost their way, and stare,
Like greyhounds, when the hare has taken the furze.
   1 *Court.* Right.
And have more troubles about them
Than a serving-man that has forgot his message
When he's come upon the place.
   2 *Court.* Yonder's the king within chasing and
     swearing,
Like an old falconer upon the first flight
Of a young hawk, when some clown
Has taken away the quarry from her ;
And all the lords stand round about him,
As if he were to be baited, with much more fear
And at much mort distance,
Than a country gentlewoman sees the lions the first
     time.
Look, he's broke loose !

Enter KING *and* Lords.

   King. Find him ; or, by Osiris' self, you are all
     traitors ;
And equally shall pay to justice ; a single man,
And guilty too, break through you all !

Enter ZIRIFF.

   Zir. Confidence,
Thou paint of women and the statesman's wisdom !
Valour for cowards, and of the guilty's innocence !
Assist me now,
Sir, send these starers off :

---

[1] [An allusion to the peculiarity of the portraits by
Titian and other old masters, that, at whatever point you
place yourself, they seem to be fixing their eyes on you.]

I have some business will deserve your privacy.

    King. Leave us.

    Iol. How the villain swells upon us !   [*Exeunt.*

    Zir. Not to punish thought, or keep it
Long upon the rack of doubt, know, sir,
That, by corruption of the waiting-woman,
The common key of secrets, I have found
The truth at last, and have discovered all.
The prince, your son, was, by Aglaura's means,
'Convey'd last night unto the cypress grove,
Through a close vault that opens in the lodgings.
He does intend to join with Carimania,
But ere he goes, resolves to finish all
The rites of love, and this night means
To steal what is behind.

    King. How good is Heav'n unto me,
That, when it gave me traitors for my subjects,
Would lend me such a servant !

    Zir. How just, sir. rather,
That would bestow this fortune on the poor ;
And where your bounty had made debt so infinite
That it grew desperate their hope to pay it——

    King. Enough of that.   Thou dost but gently
    chide
Me for a fault that I will mend ; for I
Have been too poor and low in my rewards
Unto thy virtue ; but to our business.
The question is, whether we shall rely
Upon our guards again.

    Zir. By no means, sir.
Hope on his future fortunes, or their love
Unto his person, has so sicklied o'er
Their resolutions, that we must not trust them.
Besides, it were but needless here.
He passes through the vault alone, and I
Myself durst undertake that business,
If that were all ; but there is something else
This accident doth prompt my zeal to serve you in.

I know you love Aglaura, sir, with passion,
And would enjoy her; I know besides
She loves him so that whosoe'er shall bring
The tidings of his death, must carry back
The news of hers, so that your justice, sir,
Must rob your hope.   But there is yet a way——

    King. Here, take my heart; for I have hitherto
Too vainly spent the treasure of my love.
I'll have it coin'd straight into friendship all,
And make a present to thee.

    Zir. If any part of this rich happiness,
Fortune prepares now for you, shall owe itself
Unto my weak endeavours, I've enough.
Aglaura without doubt this night expects
The prince, and why should you not[1] then
Supply his place by stealth, and in disguise?

    King. I apprehend thee, Ziriff;
But there's difficulty.

    Zir. Who trades in love must be an adventurer, sir.
But here is scarce enough to make the pleasure
      dearer,
I know the cave; your brother and myself
With Iolas (for these, we're sure, do hate him),
With some few chosen more, betimes will wait
The prince's passing through the vault; if he
Comes first, he's dead; and if it be yourself,
We will conduct you to the chamber door,
And stand 'twixt you and danger afterwards.

    King. I have conceiv'd of joy, and am grown great;
Till I have safe deliverance, time's a cripple
And goes on crutches.   As for thee, my Ziriff,
I do here entertain a friendship with thee,
Shall drown the memory of all patterns past.
We will oblige by turns, and that so thick
And fast, that curious studiers of it
Shall not once dare to cast it up, or say

---

[1] [Old copies, *You should not then.*]

By way of guess, whether thou or I
Remain the debtor, when we come to die.　　[*Exeunt.*

Enter Semanthe, Orithie, Philan, Orsames,
Lords *and* Ladies.

Ori. Is the Queen ready to come out ?
Phi. Not yet, sure; the king's brother is but
. newly entered.
Sem. Come, my lord, the song then.
Ori. The song.
Ors. A vengeance take this love ! it spoils a voice
Worse than the losing of a maidenhead.
I have got such a cold with rising
And walking in my shirt a-nights, that
A bittern whooping in a reed is better music.
Ori. This modesty becomes you as ill, my lord,
As wooing would us women; pray, put's not to it.
Ors. Nay, ladies, you shall find me
As free as the musicians of the woods
Themselves; what I have, you shall not need to call
　　for,
Nor shall it cost you anything.

SONG.[1]

Why so pale and wan, fond lover ?
　　Prithee, why so pale ?
Will, when looking well can't move her,
　　Looking ill prevail ?
　　Prithee, why so pale ?

[1] " This celebrated song forms a part of the tragedy of
Aglaura, where it is sung by Orsames. This song is one
of the few of his which are remembered. Perhaps this and
the [word illegible] are better known to the public than
any others of his. The lover's indifference is admirably
expressed."— *W. W.*

Why so dull and mute, young sinner ?
Prithee, why so mute ?
Will, when speaking well can't win her,
Saying nothing do 't ?
Prithee, why so mute ?

Quit, quit, for shame, this will not move:
This cannot take her.
If of herself she will not love,
Nothing can make her :
The devil take her !

Ori. I should have guess'd, it had been the issue of
Your brain, if I had not been told so.

Ors. A little foolish counsel, madam, I gave a friend
Of mine four or five years ago, when he was
Falling into a consumption.

Enter QUEEN.

Orb. Which of all you have seen the fair prisoner,
Since she was confin'd ?

Sem. I have, madam.

Orb. And how behaves she now herself ?

Sem. As one that had intrench'd so deep in
      innocence,
She fear'd no enemies : bears all quietly,
And smiles at Fortune whilst she frowns on her.

Orb. So gallant ? I wonder where the beauty lies,
That thus inflames the royal blood ?

Ori. Faces, madam, are like books ; those that do
      study them
Know best ; and to say truth, 'tis still
Much as it pleases the Courteous Reader.

Orb. These lovers sure are like astronomers,
That, when the vulgar eye discovers but
A sky above, studded with some few stars,
Find out, besides, strange fishes, birds, and beasts.

Sem. As men in sickness, scorched into a raving,

Do see the devil in all shapes and forms,
When standers-by, wondering, ask where and when:
So they in love : for all's but fever there,
And madness too.

Orb. That's too severe, Semanthe ;
But we will have your reasons in the park ;
Are the doors open through the gardens ?

' *Lord.* The king has newly led the way.　[*Exeunt.*

Enter ARIASPES : ZIRIFF *with a warrant sealed.*

Ari. Thou art a tyrant, Ziriff : I shall die with
joy.

Zir. I must confess, my lord, had but the prince's
ills
Proved slight, and not thus dangerous,
He should have ow'd to me—at least I would
Have laid a claim unto his safety ; and,
Like physicians that do challenge right
In nature's cures, look'd for reward and thanks ;
But, since 'twas otherwise, I thought it best
To save myself, and then to save the state.

Ari. 'Twas wisely done.

Zir. Safely, I'm sure, my lord ! you know 'tis not
Our custom, where the king's dislike once swells to
hate,
There to engage ourselves.　Court friendship
Is a cable, that in storms is ever cut,
And I made bold with it ; here is the warrant
seal'd ;
And for the execution of it, if you think
We are not strong enough, we may have
Iolas ; for him the king did name.

Ari. And him I would have named.

Zir. But is he not too much the prince's, sir ?

Ari. He is as lights in scenes at masques,
What glorious show soe'er he makes without,
I that set him there, know why and how.　.
But here he is.　　　　　　　　[*Enter Iolas.*

Come, Iolas; and since the heav'ns decreed
The man whom thou shouldst envy, should be such,
That all men else must do't, be not ashamed
Thou once wert guilty of it;
But bless them, that they give thee now a means
To make a friendship with him, and vouchsafe
To find thee out a way to love, where well
Thou couldst not hate.

    Iol. What means my lord?

    Ari. Here, here he stands that has preserved us
      all:
That sacrific'd unto a public good
The dearest private good we mortals have,
Friendship: gave into our arms the prince,
When nothing but the sword, perchance a ruin,
Was left to do it.

    Iol. How could I chide my love and my ambition
      now,
That thrust upon me such a quarrel? here I do
      vow——

    Zir. Hold, do not vow, my lord, let it deserve it
      first,
And yet (if heav'n bless honest men's intents),
'Tis not impossible. My lord, you will be pleased
T' inform him in particulars. I must be gone.
The king, I fear, already has been left too long alone.

    Ari. Stay: the hour and place.

    Zir. Eleven, under the Terrace Walk;
I will not fail you there; I had forgot.

              [*Goes out, returns back again.*
'T may be, the small remainder of those lost men,
That were of the conspiracy, will come along with
      him:
'Twere best to have some chosen of the guard
Within our call.   [*Exit Ziriff.*

    Ari. Honest and careful Ziriff!
              [*Iolas stands musing.*

How now? planet-struck!

Iol. This Ziriff will grow great with all the
world.

Ari. Shallow man, short-sighteder than travellers
in mists,

Or women that outlive themselves; dost thou not
see,

That whilst he does prepare a tomb with one hand

For his friend, he digs a grave with th' other for
himself?

Iol. How so?

Ari. Dost think he shall not feel the weight of
this,

As well as poor Thersames?

Iol. Shall we then kill him, too, at the same
instant?

Ari. And say the prince made an unlucky thrust.

Iol. Right.

Ari. Dull, dull, he must not die so uselessly.

As when we wipe off filth from any place,

We throw away the thing that made it clean,

So this once done, he's gone.

Thou know'st the people love the prince; to their
rage

Something the state must offer up. Who fitter

Than thy rival and my enemy?

Iol. Rare! our witness will be taken.

Ari. Pish! let me alone.

The giants that made mountains ladders,

And thought to take great love by force, were
fools:

Not hill on hill, but plot on plot, does make

Us sit above, and laugh at all below us. [*Exeunt.*

Enter AGLAURA *and a* Singing Boy.

Boy. Madam, 'twill make you melancholy,

I'll sing the prince's song; that's sad enough.

Agl. What you will, sir.

SONG.[1]

No, no, fair heretic, it needs must be
  But an ill love in me,
  And worse for thee.

For were it in my power,
To love thee now this hour[2]
  More than I did the last :

I would then so fall,
  I might not love at all.
Love that can flow, and can admit increase,
Admits as well an ebb, and may grow less.

True love is still the same ; the torrid zones,
  And those more frigid ones,
  It must not know.
For love, grown cold or hot,
  Is lust or friendship, not
  The thing we have.

For that's a flame would die,
Held down or up too high :

  Then think I love more than I can express,
  And would love more, could I but love thee
  less.

Agl. Leave me, for to a soul so out of tune,
As mine is now, nothing is harmony :
When once the mainspring, Hope, is fall'n into
Disorder ; no wonder if the lesser wheels,

---

[1] "This song must have been popular in its day, as it will be found copied in many of the early collections of songs."—*W. W.*

[2] "A similar thought may be found in Moore. Speaking of love, he says :—

 "That, though the heart would break with more,
  It could not live with less."
—*W. W.*

Desire and Joy, stand still; my thoughts, like bees,
When they have lost their king, wander
Confusedly up and down, and settle nowhere.

Enter ORITHIE.

Orithie, fly, fly the room,
As thou wouldst shun the habitations
Which spirits haunt, or where thy nearer friends
Walk after death. Here is not only love,
But love's plague too, misfortune; and so high,
That it is sure infectious.

    Ori. Madam, so much more miserable am I this
      way than you,
That should I pity you, I should forget myself,
My sufferings are such, that with less patience
You may endure your own, than give mine audience.
There is that difference, that you may make
Yours none at all, but by considering mine.

    Agl. O, speak them quickly then; the marriage-
      day
To passionate lovers never was more welcome,
Than any kind of ease would be to me now.

    Ori. Could they be spoke, they were not then so
      great.
I love, and dare not say I love; dare not hope,
What I desire; yet still too must desire.
And, like a starving man brought to a feast,
And made say grace to what he ne'er shall taste,
Be thankful after all, and kiss the hand,
That made the wound thus deep.

    Agl. 'Tis hard indeed; but with what unjust scales
Thou took'st the weight of our misfortunes,
Be thine own judge now.
Thou mourn'st for loss of that thou never hadst;
Or if thou hadst a loss, it never was
Of a Thersames.
Wouldst thou not think a merchant mad, Orithie,
If thou shouldst see him weep and tear his hair,

Because he brought not both the Indies home?
And wouldst not think his sorrows very just,
If, having fraught his ship with some rich treasure,
He sank i' th' very port? This is our case.

Ori. And do you think there is such odds in it?
Would heaven we women could as easily change
Our fortunes as, 'tis said, we can our minds.
I cannot, madam, think them miserable,
That have the prince's love.

Agl. He is the man then.
Blush not, Orithie; 'tis a sin to blush
For loving him, though none at all to love him.
I can admit of rivalship without
A jealousy, nay, shall be glad of it:
We two will sit, and think, and sigh,
And sigh, and talk of love and of Thersames.
Thou shalt be praising of his wit, while I
Admire he governs it so well:
Like this thing said thus, th' other thing thus done,
And in good language him for these adore,
While I want words to do't, yet do it more.
Thus will we do till death itself shall us
Divide, and then whose fate shall be to die
First of the two, by legacy shall all
Her love bequeath, and give her stock to her,
That shall survive; for no one stock can serve
To love Thersames so as he'll deserve.

Enter KING *and* ZIRIFF.

King. What, have we here impossibility?
A constant night, and yet within the room,
That that can make the day before the sun,
Silent, Aglaura, too?

Agl. I know not what you say:
Is't to your pity or your scorn I owe
The favour of this visit, sir; for such
My fortune is, it doth deserve them both?

King. And such thy beauty is, that it makes
   good
All fortunes; sorrow looks lovely here;
And there's no man that would not entertain
His griefs as friends, were he but sure they'd
   show
No worse upon him. But I forget myself;
I came to chide.

   Agl. If I have sinn'd so high,
That yet my punishment equals not my crime,
Do, sir. I should be loth to die in debt
To justice, how ill soe'er I paid
The scores of love.

   King. And those indeed thou hast but paid in-
   differently
To me. I did deserve at least fair death:
Not to be murthered thus in private.
That was too cruel, mistress.
And I do know thou dost repent, and wilt
Yet make me satisfaction.

   Agl. What satisfaction, sir?
I am no monster, never had two hearts;
One is by holy vows another's now,
And could I give it you, you would not take it,
For 'tis alike impossible for me
To love again, as you love perjury.
O sir, consider, what a flame love is!
If by rude means you think to force a light,
That of itself it would not freely give,
You blow it out, and leave yourself i' th' dark.
The prince once gone, you may as well persuade
The light to stay behind, when the sun posts
To th' other world, as me. Alas! we two
Have mingled souls more than two meeting brooks;
And whosoever is design'd to be
The murtherer of my lord (as sure there is),
Has anger'd heav'n so far, that 'twas decreed
Him to increase his punishment that way,

Would he but search the heart, when he has done,
He there would find Aglaura murthered too.
　　King. Thou hast o'ercome me, mov'd so hand-
　　　　somely
For pity, that I will disinherit
The elder brother, and from this hour be
Thy convert, not thy lover.
　　Zir. Despatch. Away!
And he that brings news of the prince's welfare,
Look that he have the same reward we had decreed
To him brought tidings of his death.
'T must be a busy and bold hand, that would
Unlink a chain the gods themselves have made:
Peace to thy thoughts, Aglaura.　　　　*[Exit.*
　　　　　　　[Ziriff steps back and speaks.
　　Zir. Whate'er he says, believe him not, Aglaura;
For lust and rage ride high within him now.
He knows Thersames made th' escape from hence,
And does conceal it only for his ends;
For by the favour of mistake and night,
He hopes t' enjoy thee in the prince's room;
I shall be miss'd, else I would tell thee more;
But thou may'st guess, for our condition
Admits no middle ways; either we must
Send them to graves, or lie ourselves in dust. *[Exit.*
　　　　　　　[Aglaura stands still and studies.
　　Agl. Ha! 'tis a strange act thought puts me now
　　　　upon;
Yet sure my brother meant the self-same thing,
And my Thersames would have done't for me:
To take his life, that seeks to take away
The life of life—honour—from me; and from
The world the life of honour—Thersames:
Must needs be something, sure, of kin to justice.
If I do fail, th' attempt howe'er was brave,
And I shall have at worst a handsome grave. *[Exit.*

Enter IOLAS, SEMANTHE.

[*Semanthe steps back, Iolas stays her.*

Iol. What, are we grown, Semanthe, night and
    day?
Must one still vanish, when the other comes?
Of all that ever love did yet bring forth
(And 't has been fruitful too) this is
The strangest issue.

    Sem. What, my lord?

    Iol. Hate, Semanthe.

    Sem. You do mistake; if I do shun you, 'tis
As bashful debtors shun their creditors.
I cannot pay you in the self-same coin,
And am asham'd to offer any other.

    Iol. It is ill done, Semanthe, to plead bankrupt,
When with such ease you may be out of debt.
In love's dominions native commodity
Is current payment; change is all the trade,
And heart for heart the richest merchandise.

    Sem. 'Twould here be mean, my lord, since mine
    would prove
In your hands but a counterfeit, and yours in mine
Worth nothing. Sympathy, not greatness,
Makes those jewels rise in value.

    Iol. Sympathy? O, teach but yours to love then,
And two so rich no mortal ever knew.

    Sem. That heart would love but ill that must be
    taught;
Such fires as these still kindle of themselves.

    Iol. In such a cold and frozen place as is
Thy breast, how should they kindle of themselves,
Semanthe?

    Sem. Ask how the flint can carry fire within!
'Tis the least miracle that love can do.

    Iol. Thou art thyself the greatest miracle,
For thou art fair to all perfection,

And yet dost want the greatest part of beauty—
Kindness. Thy cruelty (next to thyself)
Above all things on earth takes up my wonder.
   Sem. Call not that cruelty, which is our fate.
Believe me, Iolas, the honest swain,
That from the brow of some steep cliff far off,
Beholds a ship labouring in vain against
The boisterous and unruly elements, ne'er had
Less power or more desire to help than I.
At every sigh I die, and every look
Does move; and any passion you will have
But love, I have in store. I will be angry,
Quarrel with destiny and with myself,
That 'tis no better : be melancholy ;
And (though mine own disasters well might plead
To be in chief) yours only shall have place.
I'll pity, and (if that's too low) I'll grieve,
As for my sins, I cannot give you ease.
All this I do, and this I hope will prove
'Tis greater torment not to love than love.   [*Exit.*
   Iol. So perishing sailors pray to storms,
And so they hear again. So men,
With death about them, look on physicians, that
Have given them o'er, and so they turn away :
Two fixed stars, that keep a constant distance,
And by laws made with themselves must know
No motion eccentric, may meet as soon as we :
The anger that the foolish sea does show,
When it does brave it out, and roar against
A stubborn rock that still denies it passage,
Is not so vain and fruitless as my prayers.
Ye mighty powers of love and fate, where is
Your justice here ? It is thy part (fond boy),
When thou dost find one wounded heart, to make
The other so ; but if thy tyranny
Be such, that thou wilt leave one breast to hate,
If we must live, and this survive,
How much more cruel's fate ?   [*Exit.*

ACTUS V. SCŒNA I.

Enter ZIRIFF, ARIASPES, IOLAS.

Iol. A glorious night !
Ari. Pray heav'n it prove so.
Are we not there yet ?
   Zir. 'Tis about this hollow.   [*Enter the cave.*
   Ari. How now ! what region are we got into ?
Th' inheritance of night !
Are we not mistaken a turning, Ziriff,
And stept into some melancholy devil's territory ?
Sure 'tis a part of the first Chaos,
That would endure no change.
   Zir. No matter, sir, 'tis as proper for our purpose
As the lobby for the waiting-woman's.
Stay you here : I'll move a little backward ;
And so we shall be sure to put him past
Retreat.   You know the word, if't be the prince.
              [*Goes to the mouth of the cave.*

Enter KING.

Here, sir, follow me, all's quiet yet.
   King. He's not come then ?
   Zir. No.
   King. Where's Ariaspes ?
   Zir. Waiting within.
     [*He leads him on : steps behind him, gives*
       the false word : they kill the King.

   Iol. I do not like this waiting,
Nor this fellow's leaving us.
   Ari. This place does put odd thoughts into thee.
Then thou art in thine own nature, too, as jealous
As either love or honour.   Come, wear thy sword in
    readiness,
And think how near we are a crown.
   Zir. Revenge !

Lo, let us drag him to the light, and search
His pockets; there may be papers there, that will
Discover the rest of the conspirators.
Iolas, your hand.   [*Draws him out.*
   Iol. Whom have we here? the king!
   Zir. Yes, and Zorannes too.   Hallo, ho!
                  [*Enter Pasithas and others.*
Unarm them.
D'ye stare?
This for my father's injuries and mine!
         [*Points to the King's dead body.*
Half love's, half duty's sacrifice:
This for the noble prince, an offering to friendship!
                [*Runs at Iolas.*

   Iol. Basely and tamely.   [*Dies.*
   Ari. What hast thou done?
   Zir. Nothing! kill'd a traitor.
So, away with them; and leave us.
Pasithas, be only you in call.
   Ari. What, dost thou pause?
Hast thou remorse already, murtherer?
   Zir. No, fool: 'tis but a difference I put
Betwixt the crimes: Orbella is our quarrel;
And I do hold it fit, that love should have
A nobler way of justice than revenge
Or treason.   Follow me out of the wood,
And thou shalt be master of this again:
And then best arm and title take.
       [*They go out and enter again.*
There!   [*Gives him his sword.*
   Ari. Extremely good!   Nature took pains, I
   swear:
The villain and the brave are mingled handsomely.
   Zir. 'Twas fate that took it, when it decreed
We two should meet, nor shall they mingle now:
We are brought together straight to part.   [*Fight.*
   Ari. Some devil, sure, has borrowed this shape.
                 [*Pause.*

My sword ne'er stay'd thus long to find an entrance.

Zir. To guilty men all that appears is devil;
Come, trifler, come.   [*Fight again.   Ariaspes falls.*

Ari. Whither, whither, thou fleeting coward life?
Bubble of time, Nature's shame, stay a little, stay;
Till I have look'd myself into revenge,
And star'd this traitor to a carcass first.
It will not be.   [*Falls.*
The crown, the crown, too,
Now is lost, for ever lost.   O!
Ambition's but an *ignis fatuus*, I see,
Misleading fond mortality,
That hurries us about, and sets us down
Just—where—we—first—began.   [*Dies.*

Zir. What a great spreading mighty thing this
      was,
And what a nothing now! how soon poor man
Vanishes into his noontide shadow!
But hopes o'erfed have seldom better done. [*Halloes.*

Enter PASITHAS.

Take up this lump of vanity and honour,
And carry it the back way to my lodging,
There may be use of statesmen when they're dead;
So.   For the Citadel now; for in such times
As these, when the unruly multitude
Is up in swarms, and no man knows which way
They'll take, 'tis good to have retreat.   [*Exeunt.*

Enter THERSAMES.

Ther. The dog-star's got up high; it should be
      late;
And sure by this time every waking ear
And watchful eye is charm'd; and yet methought
A noise of weapons struck my ear just now!
'Twas but my fancy, sure, and were it more,
I would not tread one step that did not lead
To my Aglaura, stood all his guard betwixt,

With lightning in their hands.
Danger! thou dwarf dress'd up in giant's clothes,
That show'st far off still greater than thou art,
Go, terrify the simple and the guilty, such
As with false optics still do look upon thee.
But fright not lovers: we dare look on thee
In thy worst shape, and meet thee in them too.
Stay. These trees I made my mark; 'tis here-
 abouts,
Love, guide me but [a]right this night,
And lovers shall restore thee back again
Those eyes the poets took so boldly from thee.

[Exit.

AGLAURA, *with a torch in one hand and a dagger*
in the other.

Agl. How ill this does become this hand, how
 much the worse
This suits with this! one of the two should go.
The she within me says, it must be this:
Honour says this; and honour is Thersames' friend.
What is that she then? it is not a thing
That sets a price, not upon me, but on
Life in my name, leading me into doubt,
Which, when't has done, it cannot light me out.
For fear does drive to fate, or fate, if we
Do fly, o'ertakes, and holds us, till or death
Or infamy, or both, doth seize us.

[Puts out the light.

Ha! would 'twere in again!
Antics and strange misshapes,
Such as the porter to my soul, mine eye,
Was ne'er acquainted with, fancy lets in,
Like a distracted multitude, by some strange ac-
 cident
Piec'd together. Fear now afresh comes on,
And charges love too home.
He comes! he comes!

Woman, if thou wouldst be the subject of man's
    wonder,
Not his scorn hereafter, now show thyself.

Enter PRINCE, *rising from the vault ; she stabs him
two or three times ; he falls ; she goes back to her
chamber.*

Sudden and fortunate !
My better angel, sure, did both infuse
A strength, and did direct it.

Enter ZIRIFF.

    Zir. Aglaura !
    Agl. Brother !
    Zir. The same.
So slow to let in such a long'd-for guest ?
Must joy stand knocking, sister ? come, prepare,
    prepare :
The king of Persia's coming to you straight !
The king ! mark that.
    Agl. I thought how poor the joys you brought
    with you,
Were in respect of those that were with me.
Joys are our hopes stript of their fears,
And such are mine ; for know, dear brother,
The king is come already, and is gone.   Mark that.
    Zir. Is this instinct or riddle ? what king ? how
    gone ?
    Agl. The cave will tell you more——
    Zir. Some sad mistake : thou hast undone us all.
                         [*Goes out, enters hastily again.*
The prince, the prince ! cold as the bed of earth he
    lies
Upon, as senseless too ! death hangs upon his lips,
Like an untimely frost upon an early cherry.
The noble guest (his soul) took it so ill,
That you should use his old acquaintance so,
That neither prayers nor tears can e'er persuade

Him back again.   [*Aglaura swoons ; he rubs her.*
Hold, hold ! we cannot sure part thus !
Sister ! Aglaura ! Thersames is not dead,
It is the prince that calls.

Agl. The prince ? where ?
Tell me, or I will straight go back again
Into those groves of jessamine thou took'st me from
And find him out, or lose myself for ever.

Zir. For ever ? Ay, there's it !
For in those groves thou talk'st of,
There are so many byways and odd turnings,
Leading unto such wide and dismal places,
That should we go without a guide, or stir,
Before heav'n calls, 'tis strongly to be feared,
We there should wander up and down for ever,
And be benighted to eternity.

Agl. Benighted to eternity ?   What's that ?

Zir. Why, 'tis to be benighted to eternity,
To sit i' th' dark, and do I know not what ;
Unriddle at our own sad cost and charge
The doubts the learned here do only move.

Agl. What place have murtherers, brother, there ?
      for, sure,
The murtherer of the prince must have
A punishment that heav'n is yet to make.

Zir. How is religion fool'd betwixt our loves
And fears !   Poor girl, for ought that thou hast
      done,
Thy chaplets may be fair and flourishing,
As his in the Elysium.

Agl. Do you think so ?

Zir. Yes, I do think so.
The juster judges of our actions, would they
Have been severe upon our weaknesses,
Would, sure, have made us stronger. Fie ! those
      tears ?
A bride upon the marriage-day as properly
Might shed as thou ; here widows do't,

And marry next day after. To such a
Funeral as this there should be nothing common.
We'll mourn him so that those, that are alive,
Shall think themselves more buried far than he ;
And wish to have his grave, to find his obsequies :
But stay ; the body ?

        [Brings up the body; she swoons and dies.
Again ! sister ! Aglaura !
O, speak once more, once more look out, fair soul.
She's gone, irrevocably gone ;
And winging now the air like a glad bird
Brok'n from some cage :
Poor bankrupt heart, when 't had
Not wherewithal to pay to sad
Disaster all that was its due, it broke !
Would mine would do so too. My soul
Is now within me, like a well-mettled hawk
On a blind falc'ner's fist : methinks I feel
It baiting to be gone : and yet I have
A little foolish business here on earth.
I will despatch.   *[Exit.*

    Enter PASITHAS, *with the body of Ariaspes.*

    Pas. Let me be like my burthen, if I had not here
As lief kill two of the blood royal for him,
As carry one of them ; these gentlemen of high
Actions are three times as heavy after death, as
your private retir'd ones ; look if he be not reduc'd
to the state of a courtier of the second form now,
and cannot stand upon his own legs, nor do anything without help ? Hum ! and what's become of
the great prince, in prison as they call it now, the
toy within us, that makes us talk and laugh, and
fight : ay, why, there's it ; well, let him be what
he will, and where he will, I'll make bold with the
old tenement here. Come, sir, come along.   *[Exit.*

Enter ZIRIFF.

Zir. All's fast too here ; they sleep to-night
I' their winding-sheets, I think, there's such
A general quiet.   O, here is light, I warrant ;
For lust does take as little rest as care or age :
Courting her glass, I swear—fie ! that's a flatterer,
    madam,
In me you shall see trulier what you are.   [*Knocks.*

Enter the QUEEN.

Orb. What make you up at this strange hour, my
    lord ?
Zir. My business is my boldness' warrant, madam.
And I could well afford t' have been without
It now, had heav'n so pleas'd.
Orb. 'Tis a sad prologue :
What follows, in the name of virtue ?
Zir. The king.
Orb. Ay, what of him ? [he] is well, is he not ?
Zir. Yes.
If to be free from the great load
We sweat and labour under here on earth,
Be to be well, he is.
Orb. Why, he's not dead, is he ?
Zir. Yes, madam, slain ; and the prince too.
Orb. How ? where ?
Zir. I know not ; but dead they are.
Orb. Dead ?
Zir. Yes, madam.
Orb. Didst see them dead ?
Zir. As I see you alive.
Orb. Dead !
Zir. Yes, dead !
Orb. Well, we must all die ;
The sisters spin no cables for us mortals ;
They're Thread, and Time, and Chance.
Trust me, I could weep now ;

But wat'ry distillations do but ill on graves :
They make the lodging colder.   [*She knocks.*
   Zir. What would you, madam?
   Orb. Why, my friends, my lord,
I would consult, and know what's to be done.
   Zir. Madam, 'tis not so safe to raise the court,
Things thus unsettled : if you please to have——
   Orb. Where's Ariaspes?
   Zir. In's dead sleep by this time, I'm sure.
   Orb. I know he is not! find him instantly.
   Zir. I'm gone.   [*Turns back again.*
But, madam, why make you [a] choice of him,
From whom, if the succession meet disturbance,
All must come of danger?
   Orb. My lord, I am not yet so wise, as to
Be jealous ; pray, dispute no further.
   Zir. Pardon me, madam, if, before I go,
I must unlock a secret unto you : such a one
As, while the king did breathe, durst know no
    air—
Zorannes lives !
   Orb. Ha!
   Zir. And, in the hope of such a day as this,
Has ling'red out a life, snatching, to feed
His almost famished eyes,
Sights now and then of you in a disguise.
   Orb. Strange ! this night is big with miracle.
   Zir. If you did love him, as they say you did,
And do so still, 'tis now within your power——
   Orb. I would it were, my lord ; but I am now
No private woman. If I did love him once
(And 'tis so long ago, I have forgot),
My youth and ignorance may well excuse't.
   Zir. Excuse it?
   Orb. Yes, excuse it, sir.
   Zir. Though I confess I lov'd his father much,
And pity him, yet having offer'd it
Unto your thoughts, I have discharg'd a trust ;

And zeal shall stray no further.
Your pardon, madam.   [*Exit.   Queen studies.*
   Orb. Maybe it is a plot to keep off Ariaspes'
Greatness ; which he must fear, because he knows
He hates him : for these are statesmen ;
That, when time has made bold with king[1] and
    subject,
Throwing down all fence that stood betwixt their
    power
And others' right, are on a change,
Like wanton salmons coming in with floods,
That leap o'er wires and nets, and make their way
To be at the return to every one a prey.

   Enter ZIRIFF *and* PASITHAS ; *they throw down the
dead body of Ariaspes.*

   Orb. Ha ! murthered too !   Treason, treason !
   Zir. But such another word, and half so loud,
And thou'rt——
   Orb. Why ? thou wilt not murther me too ?
Wilt thou, villain ?
   Zir. I do not know my temper ;
                         [*Discovers himself.*
Look here, vain thing, and see thy sins full blown :
There's scarce a part in all this face thou hast
Not been forsworn by, and heav'n forgive thee
    for't !
For thee I lost a father, country, friends,
Myself almost, for I lay buried long ;
And when there was no use thy love could pay
Too great, thou mad'st the principal away.
Had I but stay'd, and not begun revenge,
Till thou hadst made an end of changing,
I had had the kingdom to have kill'd.
As wantons, ent'ring a garden, take
The first fair flower they meet, and treasure
It in their laps : then seeing more, do make

      [1] [Old copies, *the king.*]

Fresh choice again, throwing in one and one,
Till at the length the first poor flower, o'ercharg'd
With too much weight, withers and dies:
So hast thou dealt with me, and having kill'd
Me first, I'll kill——

 Orb.   Hold, hold! Not for my sake,
But Orbella's, sir, a bare and single death
Is such a wrong to justice, I must needs
Except against it.
Find out a way to make me long a-dying;
For death's no punishment: it is the sense,
The pains and fears afore, that makes a death.
To think what I had had, had I had you:
What I have lost in losing of myself,
Are deaths far worse than any you can give.
Yet kill me quickly; for, if I have time,
I shall so wash this soul of mine with tears,
Make it so fine, that you would be afresh
In love with it, and so perchance I should
Again come to deceive you.

   [She rises up weeping, and hanging down her head.
 Zir. So rises day, blushing at night's deformity:
And so the pretty flowers, blubber'd with dew,
And overwash'd with rain, hang down their heads.
I must not look upon her.   *[She goes towards him.*
 Orb. Were but the lilies in this face as fresh
As are the roses; had I but innocence
 Join'd to these[1] blushes, I should then be bold;
For when they went on begging, they were ne'er
Denied. 'Tis but a parting kiss, sir.
 Zir. I dare not grant it.
 Orb. Your hand, sir, then; for that's a part I shall
Love after death (if after death we love),
'Cause it did right the wrong'd Zorannes here

    [Steps to him, and opens the box of poison;
     Zorannes falls.

---

[1] [Old copies, *their.*]

Sleep, sleep for ever ; and forgotten too,
All but thy ills, which may succeeding time
Remember, as the seaman does his marks,
To know what to avoid.   May at thy name
All good men start, and bad too ; may it prove
Infection to the air, that people dying of it
May help to curse thee for me.

[Turns to the body of Ariaspes.

Could I but call thee back as eas'ly now !
But that's a subject for our tears, not hopes !
There is no piecing tulips to their stalks,
When they are once divorc'd by a rude hand ;
All we can do is to preserve in water
A little life, and give by courteous art,
What scanted nature wants commission for.
That thou shalt have : for to thy memory
Such tribute of moist sorrow I will pay,
And that so purifi'd by love, that on thy grave
Nothing shall grow but violets and primroses,
Of which some shall be
Of the mysterious number, so that lovers shall
Come hither, not as to a tomb, but to an oracle.

[She knocks, and raises the court.

[Enter Ladies *and* Courtiers, *as out of their beds.*

Orb. Come, come ! help me to weep myself away,
And melt into a grave ; for life is but
Repentance' nurse, and will conspire with memory
To make my hours my tortures.

Ori. What scene of sorrow's this ?   Both dead ?

Orb. Dead ?   Ay, and 'tis but half death's triumphs
    this ;
The king and prince lie somewhere, just
Such empty trunks as these.

Ori.   The prince ?
Then in grief's burthen I must bear a part.

Sem. The noble Ariaspes : valiant Ziriff too.

[Weeps.

Orb. Weep'st thou for him, fond prodigal? dost
    know,
On whom thou spend'st thy tears? This is the
    man,
To whom we owe our ills; the false Zorannes
Disguised, not lost; but kept alive by some.

Enter PASITHAS, *surveys the bodies, finds his master.*

Incensed power, to punish Persia thus!
He would have kill'd me too; but heav'n was just,
And furnish'd me with means to make him pay
His[1] score of vill'ny, ere he could do more.
    Pas. Were you his murther'r then?
            [*Pasithas runs to her, kills her, and flies.*
    Ori. Ah me! the queen!
            [*They rub her till she comes to herself.*
    Sem. How do you do, madam?
    Orb. Well; but I was better and shall—— [*Dies.*
    Sem. O, she is gone for ever!

Enter Lords *in their nightgowns,* ORSAMES, PHILAN.

    Ors. What have we here? A churchyard?
Nothing but silence and [the] grave?
    Ori. O, here has been, my lords,
The blackest night the Persian world e'er knew;
The king and prince are not themselves exempt
From this arrest; but pale and cold as these,
Have measured out their lengths.
    Lords. Impossible; which way?
    Sem. Of that we are as ignorant as you;
For, while the queen was telling of a story,
An unknown villain here has hurt her so
That, like a sickly taper, she but made
One flash, and so expir'd.
            [*Enter, bearing in Pasithas.*

---

[1][Old copies, *this.*]

Phi.　　　　　　　　　　Here he is,
But no confession.

　　Ori.　　　　　　　Torture must force him then :
Though 'twill indeed but weakly satisfy
To know, now they are dead, how they did die.

　　Phi. Come, take the bodies up, and let us all
Go drown ourselves in tears.　This massacre
Has left so torn a state, that 'twill be policy,
As well as debt, to weep till we are blind ;
For who would see the miseries behind ?

OUR play is done, and yours doth now begin :
    What different fancies people now are in :
How strange and odd a mingle it would make,
If, ere they rise, 'twere possible to take
All votes.—
But as when an authentic watch is shown,
Each man winds up and rectifies his own,
So in our very judgments. For there sits
A grave grand jury on it of town wits,
And they give up their verdict ; then again
The other jury of the court comes in
(And that's of life and death) ; for each man sees,
That oft condemns, what th' other jury frees.
Some three days hence, the ladies of the town
Will come to have a judgment of their own.
And after them, their servants ; then the city,
For that is modest, and is still last witty.
'Twill be a week at least yet, ere they have
Resolv'd to let it live, or giv't a grave.
Such difficulty there is to unite
Opinion, or bring it to be right.

SIR,

THAT the abusing of your ear's a crime,
    Above th' excuse any six lines in rhyme
Can make, the poet knows : I am but sent
T' intreat he may not be a president,[1]
For he does think, that in this place there be
Many have done't as much and more than he.
But here's, he says, the difference of the fates,
He begs a pardon after't, they estates.

[1] [Precedent.]

AGLAURA

PRESENTED AT THE COURT.

*Aglaura. Presented at the Court by His Maiesties Servants.
Written by Sir John Suckling.*

PROLOGUE.

'FORE love, a mighty sessions, and (I fear)
    Though kind last 'sizes, 'twill be now severe ;
For it is thought, and by judicious men,
Aglaura 'scap'd only by dying then.
But 'twould be vain for me now to endear,
Or speak unto my Lords, the Judges here,
They hold their places by condemning still,
And cannot show at once mercy and skill ;
For wit's so cruel unto wit, that they
Are thought to want, that find not want i' th' play.
But, ladies, you who never lik'd a plot,
But where the servant had his mistress got,
And whom to see a lover die it grieves,
Although 'tis in worse language that he lives,
Will like't, we're confident, since here will be,
That your sex ever lik'd, variety !

'TIS strange, perchance you'll think, that she
      that died
At Christmas, should at Easter be a bride :
But 'tis a privilege the poets have,
To take the long-since dead out of the grave.
Nor is this all; old heroes asleep
'Twixt marble coverlets, and six foot deep
In earth, they boldly wake, and make them do
All they did living here : sometimes more too.
They give fresh life, reverse and alter fate,
And (yet more bold) Almighty-like create,
And out of nothing, only to deify
Reason and Reason's friend, Philosophy ;
Fame, honour, valour : all that's great or good,
Or is at least 'mongst us so understood—
They give ; heav'n's theirs ; no handsome woman
      dies,
But, if they please, is straight some star i' th' skies.
But O, how those poor men of metre do
Flatter themselves with that that is not true !
And 'cause they can trim up a little prose,
And spoil it handsomely, vainly suppose
They're omnipotent, can do all those things
That can be done only by Gods and kings !
Of this wild guilt he fain would be thought free,
That writ this play, and therefore (sir) by me
He humbly begs you would be pleas'd to know,
Aglaura's but repriev'd this night ; and though
She now appears upon a poet's call,
She's not to live, unless you say she shall.

AGLAURA

PRESENTED AT THE COURT.

ACTUS V. SCŒNA I.

Enter ZIRIFF, PASITHAS, *and* GUARD : *he places 'em
and Exit. A state set out.*

Enter ZIRIFF, IOLAS, ARIASPES.

Iol. A glorious night !
Ari.   Pray Heav'n it prove so !
Are we not there yet ?
Zir.   .   'Tis about this hollow.
                    [*They enter the cave.*
  Ari. How now ! what region are we got into,
Th' inheritance of night ?
Have we not mistaken a turning, Ziriff,
And stepp'd into the confines of some melancholy
Devil's territory ?
  Iol. Sure, 'tis a part of the first Chaos,
That would not suffer any change.
  Zir. No matter, sir, 'tis as proper for our
Purpose, as the lobby for the waiting-woman's.
Stay you here ; I'll move a little backward ;
And so we shall be sure to put him past
Retreat.   You know the word, if it be the prince ?
                    [*Ziriff goes to the door.*
            Enter KING.

Zir. Here, sir, follow me ; all's quiet yet.

King. Is he not come then ?

Zir. No.

King. Where's Ariaspes ?

Zir. Waiting within.

Iol. I do not like this waiting,
Nor this fellow's leaving of us.

Ari. This place does put odd thoughts into thee.
Then thou art in thine own nature, too,
As jealous as love or honour ; wear thy sword
In readiness, and think how near we are a crown.

    Zir. Revenge !   [*Guard seizeth on 'em.*

King. Ha ! what's this ?

Zir. Bring them forth.   [*Brings them forth.*

Ari. The king !

Zir. Yes, and the prince's friend.

                      [*Discovers himself.*

D'you know this face ?

    King. Zorannes !

Zor.   The very same,
The wrong'd Zorannes ! King, d'you stare ?
Away with them, where I appointed.

    King.   Traitors !
Let me go, villain, thou dar'st not do this.

    Zor. Poor counterfeit, how fain thou now wouldst
        act a king,
And art not ! Stay you [*to Ariaspes*]. Unhand
    him [*in a whisper*].
Leave us now. [*Exeunt. Manent Ariasp. et Zoran.*

    Ari.   What does this mean ? Sure
He does intend the crown to me !

    Zor.   We are alone,
Follow me out of the wood, and thou shalt be
Master of this again ; and then best arm
And title take it !

    Ari.   Thy offer is so noble,
In gratitude I cannot but propound
Gentler conditions ; we will divide the empire.

Zor. Now, by my father's soul, I do almost repent
My first intents, and now could kill thee scurvily,
For thinking, if I'd a mind to rule, I would not rule
Alone. Let not thy easy faith (lost man)
Fool thee into so dull an heresy ;
Orbella is our quarrel, and I have thought it fit
That love should have a nobler way of justice,
Than revenge or treason.
If thou dar'st die handsomely, follow me.
[Exeunt, and enter both again.

Zor. There. [<i>Gives him his sword.</i>

Ari. Extremely good ; nature took pains, I swear,
The villain and the brave are mingled handsomely.

Zir. 'Twas fate that took it, when that it decreed
We two should meet ; nor shall they mingle now :
We are but brought together straight to part. [*Fight.*

Ari. Some devil sure has borrowed this shape,
My sword ne'er stay'd thus long to find an entrance.

Zir. To guilty men all that appears is devil ;
Come, trifler, come. [*Fight.*

Ari. Dog, thou hast it.

Zir. Why, then, it seems my star's as great as his,
I smile at thee.
[*Ariaspes pants, and runs at him to catch his sword.*
Thou now wouldst have me kill thee,
And 'tis a courtesy I cannot afford thee.
I have bethought myself, there will be use
Of thee. Pasithas, to the rest with him. [*Exit.*
[Enter Pasithas and two of the
Guard, and go out again.

Enter THERSAMES.

Ther. The dog-star's got up high ; it should be late :
And sure by this time every waking ear
And watchful eye is charm'd : and yet methought
A noise of weapons struck my ear just now.
'Twas but my fancy, sure ; and were it more,
I would not tread one step that did not lead

To my Aglaura, stood all his guard betwixt,
With lightning in their hands.
Danger, thou dwarf dress'd up in giant's clothes,
That show'st far off still greater than thou art,
Go, terrify the simple and the guilty, such
As with false optics still do look upon thee !
But fright not lovers : we dare look on thee
In thy worst shapes, and meet thee in them too.
Stay, these trees I made my mark, 'tis hereabouts.
Love, guide me but [a]right this night,
And lovers shall restore thee back again
Those eyes the poets took so boldly from thee.

[Exit.

A Taper. Table out.

Enter AGLAURA *with a torch in one hand, and a
dagger in the other.*

Agl. How ill this does become this hand ! much
   worse
This suits with this ! one of the two should go.
The she within me says it must be this :
Honour says this ; and honour is Thersames' friend.
What is that she then ? is it not a thing
That sets a price, not upon me, but on
Life in my name, leading me into doubt,
Which, when 't has done, it cannot light me out ?
For fear does drive to fate, or fate, if we
Do fly, o'ertakes and holds us, till or death,
Or infamy, or both, do seize us. [*Puts out the light.*
Ha ! would 'twere in again. Antics and strange
   misshapes,
Such as the porter of my soul—mine eye,
Was ne'er acquainted with, fancy lets in,
Like a disrouted multitude, by some strange accident
Piec'd together. Fear now afresh comes on,
And charges love too home. He comes, he comes !

[A little noise below.

Woman, if thou wouldst be the subject of man's
    wonder,
Not his scorn hereafter, now show thyself!

Enter THERSAMES *from the vaults; she stabs him
as he riseth.*

Ther. Unkindly done.
Agl. The prince's voice! defend it goodness!
Ther. What art thou that thus poorly hast
Destroy'd a life?
Agl.   O sad mistake, 'tis he!
Ther. Hast thou no voice?
Agl.   I would I had not, nor a being neither.
Ther. Aglaura? it cannot be.
Agl.   O, still believe so, sir;
For 'twas not I indeed, but fatal love.
  Ther. Love's wounds us'd to be gentler than these
    were,
The pains they give us have some pleasure
In them, and that these have not.

Enter ZIRIFF *with a taper.*

O, do not say 'twas you, for that does wound
Again: guard me, my better angel:
Do I wake? my eyes (since I was man) ne'er met
With any object gave them so much trouble,
I dare not ask neither to be satisfied,
She looks so guiltily.   [*Aside.*
  Agl. Why do you stare and wonder at a thing,
That you yourself have made thus miserable?
  Zir Good gods, and I o' the party too!   [*Aside.*
  Agl. Did you not tell me, that the king this night
Meant to attempt mine honour; that our condition
Would not admit of middle ways, and that
We must send them to graves, or lie
Ourselves in dust?
  Zir. Unfortunate mistake!   [*Ziriff knocks.*

Enter Pasithas.

I never did intend our safety by thy hands :
Pasithas, go instantly and fetch Andrages
From his bed.   How is it with you, sir?
   Ther.   As
With the besieg'd : my soul is so beset,
It does not know whether't had best to make
A desperate sally out by this port
Or not?
   Agl. Sure, I shall turn statue here!
   Ther. If thou dost love me, weep not, Aglaura :
All those are drops of blood, and flow from me.
   Zir. Now all the gods defend this way
Of expiation.   Thinkest thou thy crime,
Aglaura, would be less by adding to it?
Or canst thou hope to satisfy those powers,
Whom great sins do displease, by doing greater?
   Agl. Discourteous courtesy : I had
No other means left me than this, to let
Thersames know I would do nothing to him
I would not do unto myself, and that
Thou tak'st away.
   Ther.   Friend, bring me a little nearer,
I find a kind of willingness to say,
And find that willingness something obey'd,
My blood, now it persuades itself you did
Not call in earnest, maketh not such haste.
   Agl. O my dearest lord, this kindness is
So full of cruelty, puts such an ugliness
On what I have done, that when I look upon
It needs must fright
Me from myself, and which is more
Insufferable—I fear, from you.
   Ther. Why should that fright thee, which most
      comforts me?
I glory in it, and shall smile i' th' grave,
To think our love was such, that nothing but

Itself could e'er destroy it.

Agl. Destroy it? can it have ever end? Will
    you
Not be thus courteous, then, in the other world?
Shall we not be together there as here?

Ther. I cannot tell whether I may or not.

Agl.   Not tell?

Ther. No. The gods thought me unworthy of
    thee here.
And when thou art more pure, why
Should I not more doubt it?

Agl. Because, if I shall be more pure, I shall
Be then more fit for you. Our priests
Assure us an Elysium; and can
That be Elysium, where true lovers must not
Meet? Those powers that made our loves, did
    they
Intend them mortal, would sure have made them
Of a coarser stuff, would they not, my lord?

Ther. Pr'ythee, speak still;
This music gives my soul such pleasing business;
Takes it so wholly up, it finds not leisure to
Attend unto the summons death does make.
Yet they are loud and peremptory now,
And I can only——   *[Faints.*

Agl. Some pitying power inspire me with
A way to follow him: heart, wilt thou not
Break[1] of thyself!

Zir.   My griefs besot me.
His soul will sail out with this purple tide,
And I shall here be found staring after't,
Like a man that's too short o' th' ship, and's left
Behind upon the land.   *[She swoons.*

    Enter ANDRAGES.

O, welcome, welcome; here [he] lies, Andrages,
Alas, too great a trial for thy art.

[1] [Old copies, *Break it.*]

And. There's life in him: from whence these
    wounds?

Zir. O, 'tis no time for story.

And. 'Tis not mortal, my lord; bow him gently;
And help me to infuse this into him.
The soul is but asleep, and not gone forth.

Ther. O, O!

Zir. Hark! the prince does live.

Ther. Whate'er thou art hast given me a new[1]
    life,
And with it all my cares and miseries,
Expect not a reward: no, not a thanks.
If thou wouldst merit from me
(Yet who would be guilty of so lost an action?)
Restore me to my quietness again,
For life and that are most incompatible.

Zir. Still in despairs! I did not think till now
'Twas in the power of fortune to have robb'd
Thersames of himself; for pity, sir,
And reason live; if you will die,
Die not Aglaura's murther'd,
That's not so handsome; at least
Die not her murther'd and her murtherer too;
For that will surely follow. Look up, sir;
This violence of fortune cannot last ever:
Who knows but all these clouds are shadows
To set off fairer[2] days. If it grows blacker,
And the storms do rise, this harbour's always open.

Ther. What sayest thou, Aglaura?

Agl. What says Andrages?

And. Madam, would heaven [that] his mind
    would admit
As easy cure, as will his body![3] 'twas
Only want of blood, and two hours' rest
Restores him to himself.

Zir. And by that time,

---

[1] [Old copies, *now a.*]

[2] [Old copies, *your fairer.*]   [3] [Old copies, *his body will.*]

It may be, heaven will give our miseries some ease.
Come, sir, repose upon a bed ;
There's time enough to-day.

    Ther. Well, I will still obey,
Though I must fear it will be with me
But as it is with tortured men,
Whom states preserve only to rack again.   [*Exeunt.*

    Take off table. Enter ZIRIFF *with a taper.*

    Zir. All fast too here ! They sleep to-night
I' their winding-sheets, I think : there's such
A general quiet. O, here's light, I warrant you ;
For lust does take as little rest as care or age :
Courting her glass, I swear—fie ! that's a flatterer,
    madam,
In me you shall see trulier what you are.

                             [*He knocks.*

    Enter QUEEN.

    Orb. What make you up at this strange hour, my
    lord ?

    Zir. My business is my boldness' warrant,
    madam ;
And I could well afford t' have been without
It now, had heav'n so pleas'd.

    Orb. 'Tis a sad prologue ;
What follows, in the name of virtue ?

    Zir.   The king——

    Orb. Ay, what of him ? Is well, is he not ?

    Zir.   Yes.
If to be on's journey to the other world
Be to be well, he is.

    Orb.   Why, he's not dead, is he ?

    Zir. Yes, madam, dead.

    Orb. How ? where ?

    Zir. I do not know particulars.

    Orb.   Dead !

    Zir.   Yes, madam.

Orb. Art sure he's dead?

Zir. Madam, I know him as certainly dead,
As I know you too must die hereafter.

Orb. Dead!

Zir. Yes, dead.

Orb. We must all die.
The sisters spin no cables for us mortals.
They're Thread, and Time, and Chance.
Trust me, I could weep now;
But watery distillations do but ill
On graves, they make the lodging colder.

                            [She knocks.

Zir. What would you, madam?

Orb. Why, my friends, my lord,
I would consult, and know what's to be done.

Zir. Madam, 'tis not safe to raise the court,
Things thus unsettled; if you please to have——

Orb. Where's Ariaspes?

Zir. In his dead sleep by this time, sure.

Orb. I know he is not. Find him instantly.

Zir. I'm gone.   *[Turns back again.*
But, madam, why make you choice of him, from whom
If the succession meet disturbance, all
Must come of danger?

Orb. My lord, I am not yet so wise as to
Be jealous; pray, dispute no further.

Zir. Pardon me, madam, if, before I go,
I must unlock a secret to you; such
A one as, while the king did breathe,
Durst know no air? Zorannes lives.

Orb. Ha!

Zir. And in the hope of such a day as this
Has lingered out a life, snatching, to feed
His almost famish'd eyes, sights now and then
Of you, in a disguise.

Orb.   Strange! this night
Is big with miracle.

Zir. If you did love him,

As they say you did, and do so still ;
'Tis now within your power !

   Orb.   I would it were,
My lord ; but I am now no private woman ;
If I did love him once (as 'tis so long ago,
I have forgot), my youth and ignorance may well
Excuse't.

   Zir.   Excuse it ?
   Orb.   Yes, excuse it, sir.
   Zir. Though I confess I lov'd his father much,
And pity him, yet having offer'd it unto
Your thoughts, I have discharg'd a trust ; and zeal
Shall stray no further. Your pardon, madam.

                                      [*Exit.*

   Orb. Maybe, 'tis but a plot to keep off Ariaspes'
Greatness, which he must fear, because he knows
He hates him : for these great statesmen
That, when time has made bold with the king
And subject, throwing down all fence,
That stood betwixt their power
And others' right, are on a change,
Like wanton salmons coming in with floods,
That leap o'er wires and nets, and make their way,
To be at the return to every one a prey.

Enter ZIRIFF.

   Zir. Look here, vain thing, and see thy sins full
      blown !
There's scarce a part in all this face thou hast
Not been forsworn by, heav'n forgive thee for't !
For thee I lost a father, country, friends :
Myself almost ; for I lay buried long.
And when there was no use thy love could pay
Too great, thou mad'st the principal away.[1]

   [1] [In the margin of the copy of 1658 occurs the word
prompt, apparently as a direction to the speaker to utter
these words quickly. It is clear that it forms no part of
the text.]

As wantons, entering a garden, take
The first fair flow'r they meet, and treasure't in
Their laps; then seeing more, do make
Fresh choice again, throwing in one and one,
Till at length the first poor flower, over-charged
With too much weight, withers and dies.   So hast
Thou dealt with me, and, having kill'd me first,
I will kill——

    Orb.   Hold, hold! not for my sake, but
Orbella's, sir: a bare and single death
Is such a wrong to justice, I must needs
Except against it.
Find out a way to make me long a-dying;
For death's no punishment: it is the sense,
The pains and fears afore, that makes a death.
To think what I had had, had I had you,
What I have lost in losing of myself,
Are deaths far worse than any you can give.
Yet kill me quickly; for, if I have time,
I shall so wash this soul of mine with tears,
Make it so fine, that you would be afresh
In love with it, and so perchance I should
Again come to deceive you.

              [*She rises up weeping, and hanging
                down her head.*

    Zir. So rises day, blushing at night's deformity:
And so the pretty flowers blubber'd with dew,
And over-wash'd with rain, hang down their heads.
I must not look upon her.

              [*Queen goes towards him.*

    Orb. Were but the lilies in this face as fresh
As are the roses; had I but innocence join'd
To these blushes, I should then be bold; for when
They went a-begging, they were ne'er denied——
'Tis but a parting kiss, sir!

    Enter PASITHAS, *and* Two Guards.

Zir. I dare not grant it. Pasithas, away with
　her !　　　　　　　　　　　　　　　　[*Exeunt.*

A bed put out. THERSAMES *and* AGLAURA *on it*,
　　　　　　ANDRAGES *by.*

Ther. She wak'd me with a sigh, and yet she sleeps
Herself, sweet innocence !　Can it be sin to love
This shape ? and if it be not, why am
I persecuted thus ?　She sighs again ;
Sleep that drowns all cares, cannot, I see, charm
　love's.
Blest pillows, through whose fineness does appear
The violets, lilies, and the roses
You are stuff'd withal ! to whose softness I owe
The sweet of this repose, permit me to
Leave with you this.　See, if I have not wak'd her.
　　　　　　　　　　　　　[*Kisses them ; she wakes.*
Sure I was born, Aglaura, to destroy
Thy quiet.
　Agl.　　　Mine, my lord !
Call you this drowsiness a quiet then ?
Believe me, sir, 'twas an intruder I
Much struggled with, and have to thank a dream,
Not you, that it thus left me.
　Ther. A dream !　What dream, my love ?
　Agl. I dreamt, sir, it was day,
And the fear you should be found here——

　　　　　　　　Enter ZORANNES.

　Zor. Awake !　How is it with you, sir ?
　Ther. Well, extremely well, so well that, had I now
No better a remembrancer than pain,
I should forget I e'er was hurt, thanks to
Heav'n and good Andrages.
　Zor. And more than thanks ; I hope we yet shall
　live
To pay him.　How old's the night ?

And.   Far spent,
I fear, my lord.
    Zor.   I have a cause that should be heard
Yet ere daybreak, and I must needs entreat
You, sir, to be the judge in't.
    Ther. What cause, Zorannes?
    Zor. When you have promis'd——
    Ther. 'Twere hard I should deny thee anything.
                                    [*Exit Zorannes.*
Know'st thou, Andrages, what he means?
    And. Nor cannot guess, sirs.   [*Draw in the bed.*]
        I read
A trouble in his face, when first he left you ;
But understood it not.

    Re-enter ZORANNES, *with* KING, ARIASPES, IOLAS,
        QUEEN, *and* Two *or* Three Guards.

    Zor. Have I not pitch'd my nets like a good
        huntsman?
Look, sir, the noblest of the herd are here.
    Ther. I am astonished.
    Zor.   This place is yours.   [*Helps him up.*
    Ther. What wouldst thou have me do?
    Zor. Remember, sir, your promise,
I could do all I have to do alone ;
But justice is not justice, unless't be justly done :
Here then I will begin ; for here began my
        wrongs.
This woman, sir, was wondrous fair, and wondrous
        kind :
Ay, fair and kind ; for so the story runs.
She gave me look for look and glance for glance,
And every sigh like Echo's was return'd.
We sent up vow by vow, promise on promise,
So thick and strangely multiplied, that sure
We gave the heavenly registries their business ;
And other mortals' oaths then went for nothing.
We felt each other's pains, each other's joys :

Thought the same thought, and spoke the very
 same;
We were the same, and I have much ado
To think she could be ill, and I not be
So too, and after this, sir, all this, she
Was false, lov'd him and him; and had
I not begun revenge, till she
Had made an end of changing, I had had
The kingdom to have killed. What does this
Deserve?
 Ther. A punishment he best can make,
That suffered the wrong.
 Zor.   I thank you, sir,
For him I will not trouble you. His life is mine;
I won it fairly; and his is yours:
He lost it foully to you—
To him, sir, now:
A man so wicked that he knew no good,
But so as't made his sins the greater for't.
Those ills, which (singly acted) bred despair
In others, he acted daily, and ne'er thought
Upon them.
The grievance each particular has against him,
I will not meddle with; it were to give him a
Long life to give them hearing:
I'll only speak my own.
First then the hopes of all my youth, and a
Reward which heaven hath settled on me
(If holy contracts can do anything),
He ravish'd from me, kill'd my father—
Aglaura's father, sir, [and] would have whor'd my
 sister,
And murthered my friend. This is all!
And now your sentence, sir.
 Ther. We have no punishment can reach these
 crimes;
Therefore 'tis justest sure to send him, where
They're wittier to punish than we are here;

And 'cause repentance oft stops that proceeding,
A sudden death is sure the greatest punishment.
  Zor. I humbly thank you, sir.
  King. What a strange glass th' have showed me
    now myself
In !   Our sins, like to our shadows, when
Our day was[1] in its glory, scarce appear'd,
Towards our evening how great and monstrous
They are !
  Zor. Is this all you have to say ?   [*Draws.*
  Ther.   Hold !
Now go you up.
  Zor.   What mean you, sir ?
  Ther. Nay, I denied not you.   That all
Thy accusations are just, I must acknowledge ;
And to these crimes I have but this t'oppose—
He is my father and thy sovereign !
'Tis wickedness, dear friend, we go about
To punish ; and when we have murther'd him,
What difference is there betwixt him and
Ourselves, but that he first was wicked ?
Thou now wouldst kill him, 'cause he kill'd thy
  father ;
And when thou'st killed [him], have not I the self-
Same quarrel ?
  Zor.   Why, sir, you know you would
Yourself have done it.
  Ther.   True : and therefore 'tis
I beg his life.   There was no way for me
To have redeem'd th' intent, but by a real
Saving of it.   If he did not ravish from
Thee thy Orbella, remember that that
Wicked issue had a noble parent—love.

  [*Be ready, Courtiers and Guard, with their swords*
    drawn at the breasts of the prisoners.

Remember how he lov'd Zorannes, when

    [1] [Old copies, *is.*]

He was Ziriff! There's something due to that.
If you must needs have blood for your revenge,
Take it here. [*Offers his breast.*] Despise it not,
    Zorannes.   [*Zorannes turns away.*
The gods themselves, whose greatness makes
The greatness of our sins, and heightens 'm, above
What we can do unto each other, accept
Of sacrifice for what we do 'gainst them.
Why should not you? and 'tis much thriftier too :
You cannot let out life there, but my honour
Goes ; and all the life you can take here,
Posterity will give me back again ;
See, Aglaura weeps !
That would have been ill rhetoric in me,
But where it is, it cannot but persuade.
    Zor. Th' have thaw'd the ice about my heart ; I
      know
Not what to do.
    King. Come down, come down :
I will be king again.
There's none so fit to be the judge of this
As I. The life you show'd such zeal to save
I here could willingly return you back ;
But that's the common price of all revenge.

Enter Guard, ORSAMES, PHILAN, Courtiers, ORITHIE,
          SEMANTHE.

    Iol. Ari. Ha, ha, ha ! how they look now !
    Zor. Death : what's this ?
    Ther.   Betray'd again !
All th' ease our fortune gives our misery[1] is hope,
And that, still proving false, grows part of it.
    King. From whence this guard?
    Ari.   Why, sir, I did corrupt,
While we were his prisoners,
One of his own to raise the court.

           [1] [Old copies, *miseries.*]

Shallow souls! that thought we could not counter-
 mine!
Come, sir, you're in good posture to despatch them.
 King. Lay hold upon his instrument. Fond
 man!
Dost think I am in love with villainy?
All the service they can do me here is but
To let these see the right I do them now
Is unconstrain'd: then thus I do proceed:—
Upon the place Zorannes lost his life
I vow to build a tomb; and on that tomb
I vow to pay three whole years' penitence;
If in that time I find, that heaven and you
Can pardon, I shall find again the way
To live amongst you.
 Ther. · Sir, be not so cruel
To yourself; this is an age.
 King. 'Tis now irrevocable;
Thy father's lands I give thee back again, and his
 commands;
And with them leave to wear the tiara
That man there has abus'd. To you, Orbella,
Who, it seems, are foul as well as I,
I do prescribe the self-same physic I
Do take myself; but in another place
And for a longer time—Diana's nunnery.
 Orb. Above my hopes. [*Aside.*
 King. [*To Ari.*] For you, who still have been
The ready instrument of all my cruelties,
And there have cancell'd all the bonds of brother,
Perpetual punishment! Nor, should this line
 expire,
Shall thy right have a place.
 Ari. Hell and furies! [*Exit.*
 King. [*To Zir.*] Thy crimes deserve no less; yet,
 'cause thou wert
Heaven's instrument to save my life,
Thou only hast the time of banishment

I have of penitence.

   [Comes down. Ziriff offers to kiss the king's hand.

   Iol.   May it be plague

And famine here, till I return. No : thou shalt not

Yet forgive me.

   King. Aglaura, thus I freely part with thee,

And part with all fond flames and warm desires.

I cannot fear new agues in my blood, since I

Have overcome the charms thy beauty had :

No other ever can have so much pow'r.

Thersames, thou look'st pale ! Is't want of rest ?

   Ther. No, sir ; but that's a story for your ear.

                         [They whisper.

   Ors. A strange and happy change.

   Ori. All joys wait on you ever.

   Agl. Orithie,

How for thy sake now could I wish love were

No mathematic point, but would admit

Division, that Thersames might, though at

My charge, pay thee the debt he owes thee.

   Ori. Madam, I loved the prince, not myself.

Since his virtues have their full rewards,

I have my full desires.

   King. What miracles of preservation have we had ?

How wisely have the stars prepar'd you for felicity ?

Nothing endears a good more than the contemplation

Of the difficulty we had to attain to it :

But see, night's empire's out !

And a more glorious auspiciously does begin ;

Let us go serve the gods, and then prepare

For jollity. This day I'll borrow from my vows.

Nor shall it have a common celebration ;

Since it must be

A high record to all posterity.   *[Exeunt omnes.*

EPILOGUE.

PLAYS are like feasts, and every act should be
    Another course, and still variety :
But, in good faith, provision of wit
Is grown of late so difficult to get
That, do we what we can, we are not able
Without cold meats to furnish out the table.
Who knows but it was needless too ? maybe,
'Twas here, as in the coachman's trade ; and he
That turns in the least compass shows most art,
Howe'er, the poet hopes, sir, for his part,
You'll like not those so much who show their skill
In entertainment, as who show their will.

END OF VOL. I.

PRINTED BY JAMES BELL AT THE PRIORY PRESS,
48, ST. JOHN'S SQUARE, CLERKENWELL, E.C.